# Death at the Green Man

Veronica Vale Investigates - book 8

## Kitty Kildare

K.E. O'Connor Books

Copyright © 2025 by Kitty Kildare

All rights reserved. No part of this publication may be reproduced, distributed, or transmitted in any form or by any means, including photocopying, recording, or other electronic or mechanical methods, without the prior written permission of the publisher, except as permitted by U.S. copyright law.

For permission requests, contact: kittykildare@kittykildare.com

The story, all names, characters, and incidents portrayed in this production are fictitious. No identification with actual persons (living or deceased), places, buildings, and products is intended or should be inferred.

ISBN: 978-1-915378-93-4

DEATH AT THE GREEN MAN

Book Cover by Victoria Cooper

# Chapter 1

"This is the fourth woman he's interacted with in the last hour. Just what kind of rascal are we dealing with?" I paused in the doorway of a small shop selling a variety of seaside treats, from buckets and spades to sticks of rock with a bright pink glaze.

Benji, my ever-loyal four-legged companion, stood beside me, his nose in the air, enjoying the tempting scents from the nearby fish and chip shop.

"His wife is right to suspect him," I muttered. "One of these women must be the mistress. Let's hope they aren't all mistresses, or the man will need the constitution of a stallion."

I took more photographs to take back to my client, Mrs Porthaven. I was under her employ after she'd grown suspicious of her younger, handsome husband when he kept finding reasons to be out of the house on weekends and evenings.

We'd followed Mr Porthaven for over an hour. I was content to walk, although I resented the frequent stops. This chatty individual insisted on talking to everyone and appeared to know all of Faversham.

Faversham was an attractive Kentish town built on a tidal creek, with a vibrant water community. It had a fascinating smuggling history. I was here for a change of scene and some restorative fresh air. After all, one can only have so many shocks before things become unpleasant.

Faversham was a forty-minute train ride from the new private investigation firm I'd established with my companion, Jacob Templeton. As business grew, our work took us further afield, and I'd barely stopped since departing London to spend more time with Jacob.

Although the amount of work we both had meant we barely saw each other. And since I was lodging in a charming bed-and-breakfast in Faversham to conduct business, my free time was sparse.

Benji nudged my leg with his nose. Mr Porthaven was on the move. His blonde lady friend clasped his arm as she giggled at something he said.

I took a quick photograph using my portable camera. Mrs Porthaven could identify the scoundrel's mistress and throw him out. She was the one with the most to lose when they parted, so she needed a legitimate reason to serve him divorce papers.

When you allow your heart to rule your head, this is what you get. You fasten yourself to an attractive fellow and leave all dignity behind.

Although the chap I'd attached myself to was jolly handsome, Jacob had a sensible head on his shoulders, and I respected him for allowing me to progress our relationship at a relaxed amble.

A woman pushing a large navy pram almost ran over my toes, and I jumped out of the way. Tucked inside the pram were wide-eyed twins, both with a dark shock of hair. The mother glared at me as if I'd been about to cause harm to her precious infants.

I mumbled an apology, frowning. I turned and almost collided with a woman holding a child's hand. Why were there suddenly so many children everywhere? I checked the time and tutted. Surely, children should be home preparing for bed, not getting under my feet.

"Let's hurry, Benji." I turned my attention to the case at hand. I wasn't thinking about infants of any age or description. Especially not Ruby Smythe's unborn child.

When I'd discovered my best friend wasn't missing, but happy and radiant, hiding in Lady M's home, I'd been stunned. Ruby was concealing a pregnancy from me, and she'd recruited Lady M to lie for her.

I shook my head. No, I wasn't thinking about that. Ruby had made her decision, and as foolish as that was, it was too late to change anything. All I could control was how I kept myself occupied and not dwell on the devastating realisation that my best friend didn't trust me with such an enormous secret.

Benji kept pace with me as we walked past the bustling cafés serving the evening trade. His tail was up, and he was always happy when on a walk, but he kept glancing at me, suggesting he knew all was not well with my constitution.

It did no good to aggravate my dear dog. He was the most loyal friend around. Much more loyal than my so-called best friend. Ruby knew I wouldn't judge her for this unfortunate situation. I had an open mind and a curious nature.

I would, naturally, demand the name of the chap involved and ensure he did right by Ruby, but I wouldn't blame her. She was a free spirit, always wearing her heart on her sleeve. There was always a risk this would happen.

Perhaps it was Alfonso, the Italian cad she'd almost walked down the aisle with. Perhaps their passion boiled over, and this infant was the result. If so, I'd track him down in Italy and demand he make an honest woman of Ruby.

A cold realisation sank into my stomach. That was why Ruby hadn't shared her news. I could be a tad overzealous when righting wrongs, and this was certainly one wrong I wouldn't leave unresolved. No man should abandon a woman in such a situation.

Unless Ruby didn't want Alfonso in her life. He'd broken her heart when he'd not shown up for their wedding. But she should still have told me. I would help. I had zero experience with motherhood, but I'd nurtured plenty of abandoned pups. It couldn't be that difficult.

"This won't do. I must focus." I'd been so ensconced in my maudlin musings that I'd lost sight of Mr Porthaven. "Drat! Where did he go?"

Benji hurried ahead, heading towards the fish and chip shop, rather than following our target.

"We'll have supper later," I said, although all the fresh air had worked up an appetite.

We'd been in Kent for almost a month, with weekly trips back to London to collect work from my uncle at the London Times, ensuring I stayed on top of my obituary correspondence. And, of course, I needed to check on my ever-ailing mother and my brother, Matthew.

Although they both kept shooing me back to Kent. Matthew now spent more time outdoors with his dog, Felix, and my mother was either writing to her new friend, Colonel Basil Griffin, or wondering if it was appropriate to invite him to visit again. Their first visit had gone splendidly. I hadn't seen so much colour in her cheeks for years.

Benji stopped outside the fish and chip shop and refused to move, his nose pointed at the door.

"Yes, it smells delicious. I'll treat you to a saveloy later," I said.

He refused to move.

"Come away," I ordered.

Benji remained where he was.

It was most unlike Benji to ignore me, and that got my attention. I peered through the large glass windows into the fish and chip shop. Mr Porthaven and his attractive blonde companion were ordering at the counter.

"Oh, you clever boy." I gave him a hearty pat and fed him a treat from my jacket pocket.

I took a few photographs of the couple at the counter. They seemed friendly, although not necessarily romantic. However, Mr Porthaven's lady friend still clasped his arm as they waited for their food.

Perhaps it was time for a packet of chips. I winked at Benji. "You wait here, and I'll get you a saveloy for being such an excellent fellow."

I pushed open the door, and the intense aroma of the chip shop surrounded me. Plenty of local fish was on the menu, but I decided to treat myself to a battered sausage with a portion of chips to share with Benji and, of course, I wouldn't forget his promised saveloy.

As I waited to place my order, I inched closer to Mr Porthaven and his companion, eager to overhear their evening plans. Unfortunately, my ability to remain discreet appeared as flawed as my ability to be a suitable best friend to Ruby, because Mr Porthaven turned and looked at me.

"May I help you with something?" he asked.

I pretended to be startled by his interest. "I was wondering about the pickled eggs. Are they fresh?"

"They look fresh from where I'm standing," the woman said. She had an East End London accent and a broad smile. "I can't stand them things. They block me up something terrible."

"Miriam, that's hardly appropriate," Mr Porthaven said. "You must excuse my cousin."

"Cousin?" I echoed in surprise. "You look nothing alike."

"We used to look similar when we were children," Miriam said. "Then this one gets a fancy job, a new haircut and suit, and barely spends more than five minutes a year with us. I practically had to twist his arm to get an invitation here."

"That's nonsense. I know how busy you are," Mr Porthaven said. "You have five children. You can hardly abandon them for a jolly by the water."

"I wouldn't have abandoned anybody if you came to see us." Miriam sniffed. "Of course, the East End's not somewhere you enjoy, though it was good enough when you were growing up."

"That's quite enough," Mr Porthaven muttered, shooting an apologetic look my way.

"You should see him now," Miriam said to me. "He's a proper man about town. Knows everyone. And even if he doesn't know them, he stops to chat, so he's best friends with them five minutes later."

"How fascinating." Was I mistaken in my assumption that Mr Porthaven was a cad and I'd been following a man who simply had a cheerful disposition? He had spoken to plenty of people, not just the attractive women.

"I'd pass on the pickled eggs if I were you," Miriam said. "The crab cakes here are the best in town, though. I always have them when I visit."

"They're the best in the county." The server handed over a newspaper-wrapped parcel. Mr Porthaven paid, and they bid me goodbye.

Perhaps there was nothing to this case. But as experience showed, it was rare to truly know a person's nature, especially when the chips were down and secrets needed hiding.

Speaking of chips, Benji would be getting restless for his supper. I paid for the food and headed outside.

We walked along the pleasant high street, the pavement busy with people bustling home from work. I broke the saveloy into small pieces and fed some to Benji as we walked. It wasn't proper manners to eat in the street, but there was something comforting about strolling along with a warm packet of chips in hand, my loyal dog by my side.

We stopped outside the second reason I was in Faversham. The Green Man pub. It was a family concern and had been part of our business for over a decade. My father had purchased it when he took a fancy to its wooden-beamed ceilings and large open fireplaces that sat at either end of the pub.

I carefully balled up the greasy newspaper and tucked it inside a waste bin before heading inside to meet Jacob. He was already at the bar, two drinks in front of him. A pint of ale for himself and a gin fizz for me.

He greeted me with a kiss and patted Benji on the head. "Did Mr Porthaven reveal his true colours?"

"We may be on a hiding to nothing with that one." I took an appreciative sip of my gin fizz. "I found no caddish behaviour. Mr Porthaven is perhaps too flirtatious for a married man, but the last woman he was with was his cousin."

"Do you have enough evidence to quell Mrs Porthaven's concerns?" Jacob asked.

"Plenty of photographs. I'll meet with her tomorrow and go over things. That will set her mind at rest." I was about to say more when a familiar voice cut through the hum of conversation.

"That's not something I can help with!" Colin Winters, my most capable landlord, loomed over a smartly dressed man in a dark business suit who stood resolutely in front of him.

"You've let me into the tunnel plenty of times," the man said.

Colin glanced at me. He was a hulking man in his early forties, the epitome of a grizzled old Navy sea dog, with a patchy grey beard and only one eye. He must appear terrifying to anyone who met him in a dark alley.

But the slightly built, well-dressed man confronting him appeared fearless. Or simply foolish.

"Is something the matter?" I asked from my position at the bar.

"I don't want to bother you, Miss Vale," Colin said gruffly. "Mr Blackwood was leaving."

"Surely we can come to a suitable arrangement," Mr Blackwood pressed, ignoring Colin's scowl and fisted hands.

"What agreement do you seek?" I asked.

"I've already said I won't help," Colin said. "He's getting obsessed, and it's unhealthy."

"Obsessed about what?" I collected my drink and gestured for Jacob to follow.

Colin heaved a sigh and jabbed a finger at Mr Blackwood. "I only let him down there a few times, and now he won't leave it alone. He wants access to the old smuggler tunnels."

"Oh! My father mentioned those. Don't they lead out to the tidal creek? They were used to transport stolen goods inland, weren't they?" I asked.

"That's right." Mr Blackwood eyed me with interest. "I've met few outsiders who know about our smuggling tunnels."

"Miss Vale owns the license to the Green Man. You're speaking to my employer, so be bleedin' polite," Colin said.

Mr Blackwood adjusted his tie. "My goodness, a thousand apologies, my dear lady. Edmund Blackwood at your service. I would have come to you if I'd known you were here. I thought it was a chap who owned this place."

"My father," I said. "He died some years ago, and the business passed to me."

"Extraordinary!" he exclaimed. "Of course, you see plenty of female landladies, but never a lady pub owner. These modern times. How marvellous!"

"Indeed they are," I said, a faint smile on my lips. "What business are you seeking to make with Colin?"

"Please, call me Edmund. I'm in desperate need of assistance," Mr Blackwood, Edmund, said.

"You're in desperate need of a clout around the ears," Colin muttered. "Stop bothering us. Go home."

Edmund ignored him, his pale blue eyes bright with excitement. He turned to me, his expression earnest. "I call on your fair-mindedness and kindness to help me in a most desperate matter."

I glanced at Jacob, who looked at the man with mild exasperation.

"What would that urgent matter be?" I asked.

Edmund drew in a breath. "Finding the lost treasure of the Blackwood estate."

# Chapter 2

"There is treasure hidden beneath my pub?" Despite Edmund's earnest tone, I couldn't hide my disbelief.

"I promise you, plenty of treasure," Edmund said.

"He's talking nonsense." Colin returned to stand behind the bar, a scowl on his grizzled face.

"I assure you, every word I speak is the truth," Edmund said. "I have records! Old notes from family members. Even a map."

"Your family smuggled goods through this pub?" I asked.

Edmund had the good grace to blush, but his enthusiasm barely dimmed. "I've not followed in my ancestors' footsteps, but the information they left behind is fascinating."

"Where did you find this information?" I enquired.

"I was sorting through my parents' home after they passed away," Edmund said. "They never liked to throw anything out, so there were decades of what I thought was rubbish to sort through. It was anything but. There was an old chest in the loft, and when I pried it open, I discovered reams of paper, full of notes about smuggling routes."

"What did they bring through these tunnels?" I asked.

"Don't let his stories carry you away," Colin said. "We've all heard them, and it's the stuff of fiction."

"Colin has a point," Jacob murmured. "Ever since I've been here, I've heard tales of dark deeds involving smuggling. If they were all true, the town is overflowing with stolen gold and silver."

Colin grunted. "You're not far off the mark. Much of this town's fortune was built on illegal trading. But that doesn't mean what Mr Blackwood is saying is true."

"I've spent months researching my ancestors' claims," Edmund said. "But there's much more. A lot of information was hidden and the treasure never recovered. Some of my smuggling ancestors met a sticky end when they were caught before they could find a buyer."

"This town didn't look kindly on smugglers," Colin said. "There's a stone in the town centre, listing the names of people caught for their misdeeds. They were all hanged. And quite rightly so. You shouldn't build your fortune on crime."

"I'm not building my fortune on anything deceitful," Edmund said. "I'm already a self-made man."

"I'd like to see this tunnel," I said.

"And I'd be happy to show it to you, my dear lady," Edmund said. "But your landlord is blocking my access."

"You don't want to go into the tunnels," Colin said to me. "They're dark and damp, and it's easy to twist an ankle down there."

"I'd be happy to pay for more lighting to be installed," Edmund said. "I've said so several times."

"We can rustle up torches or candles," I said.

"You don't believe him, do you?" Jacob muttered in my ear.

"Even if it is tall tales, don't you find it exciting?" I asked. "Imagine the shenanigans that went on underneath our feet."

"It wasn't an adventure when the smugglers were caught and hanged," Jacob said. "I'm sure that list of smugglers on the stone is long."

"You're no fun." I lightly squeezed his arm.

Jacob sighed. "Very well. Let's look."

Ten minutes later, with a light in hand, Colin took us to the cellar entrance. "The smuggling tunnel is at the back, tucked away. It's easy to miss, which I suppose is the whole point."

"You won't miss anything with me leading," Edmund said. "I could walk this route with my eyes closed. In fact, I have when the candles snuffed out. Go slow and steady, and we'll be fine."

I stayed back with Colin as Edmund eased aside wooden crates stacked on top of one another, getting the occasional warning from Colin to be careful.

"Do you have a particular reason you don't want Edmund to keep investigating these tunnels?" I murmured to him.

"He's a nuisance," Colin muttered. "I only let him down there the first time because he's respectable. He's the local bank manager, and everyone thinks kindly of him. I did him a favour. Which I regret. He's here almost every day, wanting to go into the tunnel, often in the evening when it's busy. I have him to monitor and the customers. I should never have allowed it."

"Do you think there's any truth to treasure being hidden in the tunnels?"

Colin snorted. "It would have been found years ago. I understand the man needing excitement, since pushing papers around a desk and dealing with other people's money can't bring much joy, but Mr Blackwood needs to find his excitement elsewhere."

"You're a good man for letting him indulge his fantasy," I said. "And don't worry, I'll keep an eye on Edmund. If he gets pushy, I'll have a stern word and send him packing."

Colin chuckled. "I've no doubt you would. I need to get back to the bar before the customers protest they're dying of dehydration."

I nodded my thanks to him, watching as he cast a stern eye over Edmund before leaving.

"How many tunnels are there?" Jacob asked as he peered into the gloomy passageway.

"There were dozens," Edmund said. "Most have collapsed over the years. They weren't built for long-term use. Smugglers would dig a route and use it until others found it, then they'd leave it to collapse or blow it up."

"Is this one safe?" I asked.

"My ancestors knew what they were doing. They shored up most of the sections, and those they hadn't, I've made sure there's no chance of collapse."

"How long is the tunnel?" Jacob asked.

"It stretches just under a mile. You come out on the creek bank. It's a perfect location. There's a flat ridge where the boats could dock and unload. Despite my ancestors' less-than-legal behaviour, they were clever. Shall I lead the way?"

"Please do," I said. "I find this fascinating."

Edmund beamed at me. "As do I. And I'm determined to find what they hid. They were so successful that they had stores of illegal goods and couldn't sell it all at once for fear of drawing too much attention."

"You mentioned treasure," Jacob said as he took the rear, Benji between us. "Are we talking jewels?"

Edmund held aloft his torch as he made his way along the narrow, damp tunnel, the rough floor stone uneven. "They made a lot of their money on tobacco and alcohol. There are also notes mentioning opium and tea."

"None of that would have survived here for such a long time," I said.

"I believe various businesses, or wealthy individuals, immediately bought the perishable items," Edmund said. "Watch your footing. You don't want to turn your ankle."

We took our time navigating the rough floor. Benji enjoyed sniffing all the crevices. If anyone could locate this hidden treasure, it would be him.

Edmund continued, "What piqued my interest was Billy Blackwood's account of a huge haul of treasure they recovered from a coach."

"Stole, you mean?" Jacob said.

"Well, yes. Apparently, he got lucky and found a broken-down horse and carriage. To begin with, they offered help."

"Your ancestor didn't work alone?" I asked.

"No. There was a group of chaps."

"A gang," Jacob said.

"You could call them that," Edmund said. "They realised the coach carried a vast stash of gold coins and precious jewels. According to his notes, there were only three guards with the coach, so they were easy to deal with."

"Murder?" I asked.

"I... I hope not. His note didn't say."

"Good gracious," I said. "Did they mention who the coins and jewels belonged to?"

"There was a crest on the chest suggesting a royal connection," Edmund said.

"Rather than helping, they stole from this party and hauled the jewels here?" There was a note of disapproval in Jacob's voice. He was a law-abiding man, even though retired from the police.

Edmund glanced over his shoulder. "It was a different time. Men had to be inventive to make their fortune. My ancestors came from little. I can't imagine what they'd think about me working in a bank. But thanks to them, we found our footing."

"Your parents profited from their plunder?" I asked.

"Thanks to the smuggling activities, there was money, which meant my parents could buy a home and furnish it well. I wanted for nothing growing up and could have my pick of professions."

We walked a short distance in silence.

"The tunnel bends to the left as we head towards the creek bank," Edmund continued. "Mind your heads. It gets lower but wider. You'll note the passage is wide enough to bring items through on wheels to make transport easier. My ancestors thought of everything."

"Clearly not their morals," Jacob muttered to me.

Progress was slow as we made our way along the tunnel, Edmund pointing out areas he'd already investigated and explaining his plans for further excavation. He was a clever man, but I felt sceptical that the gold or jewels existed. His ancestors wouldn't have forgotten it. They must have sold it or moved it somewhere more secure.

I shivered as the damp and cold seeped through my clothes and was glad when the tunnel sloped up. A few minutes later, we emerged directly onto a flat bank, just as Edmund had described, and looked out over the low tidal creek that swept through Faversham, surrounded by land with not another person or house in sight.

"It's quite something, isn't it?" Edmund said. "All these years, and this place has barely changed. Of course, you can't build on this site because the houses would sink. It's perfect isolation for smuggling."

"I see why it makes such an excellent spot," I said.

"And you can walk from here to the pub," Edmund added. "If you squint, you should see the pub's roof to the east."

I took my time looking around. It was a beautiful setting, still claimed by nature.

"All I need is more time to find what my family hid," Edmund said. "I'll be no bother, and I'll even pay to work in the tunnels."

I considered his request. It wasn't unreasonable. "There's no need for money to exchange hands, but I ask you don't bother Colin. The Green Man is a thriving pub, and he's often shorthanded."

"I'll stay out of his way. Although I'd appreciate a key to the cellar," Edmund said. "That way, I can come and go without getting under his feet."

"Let me think about it on the walk back," I said. "We'll stay above ground this time."

Edmund clasped his hands together and drew in a breath as if to protest, but then he lowered his head and nodded.

The route back to the pub along the marshes was beautiful. Benji was delighted, happily sniffing and investigating his surroundings as we strolled beneath the darkening sky. By the time we reached the pub, the place was bustling. All the tables were taken, so we settled for stools at the bar.

"If it would convince you, you can read the notes I found," Edmund said as he ordered a round of drinks. "They detail everything my ancestors did. Their smuggling operations, their hauls. They were meticulous."

"Not meticulous enough to maintain records of where the gold and jewels were hidden," Jacob said dryly.

"You're not bothering these nice people with your stories, are you, Edmund?" A narrow-faced woman with greying hair, wearing tartan trousers and a man's waistcoat over a crisp white shirt, smirked at him.

"You know there's truth in what I'm saying, May," Edmund said. "I've even shown you some notes."

"Written by an unreliable narrator of dubious origins," the woman, May, retorted.

"What do you know about it?" Edmund muttered.

"Quite a lot." She stuck out her hand for me to shake. "May Shaw. I run the local historical society. We have authenticated documents about the smuggling that went on in this town. Edmund's so-called notes aren't among them."

I shook her hand and introduced myself, Benji, and Jacob.

"You don't have my notes because I won't let you keep them," Edmund said. "I know what you'll do. You want my treasure to lock in a cabinet and become a museum curiosity."

May lifted her eyes to the ceiling. "There is no treasure! We've found a few trinkets over the years during excavations, but the gold and jewels you claim still exist? Nothing but a fabrication."

"I'll prove you wrong," Edmund said. "And Miss Vale is helping me."

May arched an eyebrow, her gaze sweeping over me. "Is that so?"

"We've just been exploring the tunnel beneath this pub. You really don't think there's anything to the story?" I asked.

May sighed. "The history of this town has fascinated me since I was a child, but there's nothing to it. I've even written papers on the subject and submitted them for publication."

"They won't publish anything by you," Edmund scoffed. "You're not qualified."

"I will be soon," May said. "Now universities have opened slots for women, I shall attend in the autumn. I'll have my degree in three years."

"How marvellous!" I said. "I thoroughly support women getting a comprehensive education. Have you been accepted yet?"

"I have applications in for Cambridge and Oxford," May said with a hint of pride. "They'll be interested in my research. I even plan on publishing a book."

"Excuse me, Mr Blackwood." A nervous-looking young man of around twenty-five approached. He wore an ill-fitting suit and shoes that could do with a shine.

"Not now, William," Edmund said curtly. "I'm in the middle of something important."

"I need to talk to you, sir," William insisted. "This is also important."

"It'll wait until the morning when we're at work," Edmund said. "Off you go. Stop bothering me."

William shifted his weight from foot to foot, tugging at the hem of his jacket. "I really need to—"

"Tomorrow, man," Edmund snapped, his glare making William flinch.

The young man hesitated before retreating, his shoulders hunched as he scurried away to join an attractive blonde lady with a sour expression on her face.

"My apologies," Edmund said. "He's an employee at the bank, but not for much longer."

"Has he done something wrong?" I asked.

"He's not reliable and can't be trusted. That's all I can tell you about the matter." Edmund turned to me, a hopeful smile on his face. "Now, Miss Vale, what do you say? Do I have your permission to continue searching the tunnels?"

I glanced at Jacob. He discreetly shook his head, but I was intrigued. I enjoyed a good mystery.

"Very well," I said. "But on one condition. I'd like to join you in your search."

"Oh... oh, I don't know about that," Edmund stammered. "As you saw, the tunnel is no place for a lady. It's cold and damp. You could catch a chill."

"I'm perfectly capable in all situations," I replied. "And I'd be interested in doing a small excavation of my own. I'm not treasure hunting, just curious."

Edmund's brow furrowed. "I can keep anything I find?"

My gaze narrowed. "Not so fast. If we uncover anything, I'll want fifty per cent of any finds you sell. I'm helping a newly established dog rescue centre, and we're short on funds."

"Fifty! I can't agree to that."

May chortled. "You have no choice, Edmund."

He sighed. "Well, I suppose it is for a good cause."

"It's an excellent cause," I said. "If you agree, we may use the pub's office snug as our base of operations. It can be our lair, and we'll solve this mystery together. What do you think?" I met his gaze steadily, waiting for his response.

After a second of hesitation, Edmund's lips curled into a smile. He extended his hand. "I think we have a deal."

I took his hand, shaking firmly. "Then let's find this treasure, Mr Blackwood."

# Chapter 3

"Do make yourself comfortable." I pointed to a chair in the office I shared with Jacob.

Mrs Porthaven settled primly on the edge of the chair. She wore a sensible outfit of brown and beige and clutched a small leather handbag on her knee. She was well turned out, her hair pulled back into a neat bun that rested at the base of her neck. Her face was clean of makeup, her eyes bright with tension.

"I was surprised to receive your telephone call so swiftly," Mrs Porthaven said. "Was my husband so easy to unmask as a cheat?"

"You'll be glad to hear quite the opposite," I said. "I spent the best part of two days discreetly following his movements to ascertain if your fears about his unfaithfulness held."

"I'm sure they did," Mrs Porthaven said. "I was fooled by a handsome face, but his true colours came out once he was settled into the role of my husband. He assured me he'd find gainful employment but has yet to lift a finger to do so."

"I sec. And you've grown weary of him leaning on your generous nature. You hoped to find cause to remove him from the marital home with the least trouble?"

"Wouldn't you, if your chap was a worthless layabout, and his only value was a perfect smile and the dimples he flashed whenever he desired something?"

I gently sighed. "I followed your husband, and although he is an incorrigible flirt, he did nothing to discredit your matrimony vows."

"What about the women he's always seen with?" Mrs Porthaven asked. "I am a laughingstock. When I walk into Bridge Club, the other ladies snigger behind their handkerchiefs. I haven't attended a meeting for a month because I'm the source of unfounded gossip. At least if my husband was unfaithful, they'd have something suitable to fill their gossiping mouths with and perhaps offer me a crumb of sympathy."

"These are the photographs I took when I followed your husband." I presented her with the photographs of the four women Mr Porthaven spent most of his time with.

She peered at them, her nose wrinkled. "Was there canoodling?"

"None."

"I'm unable to believe that. My husband can't keep his hands to himself when he sees a pretty young thing he likes the look of."

"I'll admit sometimes his behaviour wasn't appropriate, but he did nothing so scandalous that it would bring your marriage into disrepute."

Mrs Porthaven sniffed. "You're mistaken. Keep searching. Find his mistress. I thought you were the right woman for the job, and we had an understanding about what I expected from you."

"I clearly understood the job you requested me to do," I said. "You needed your husband followed, because you feared he was straying outside the bounds of your marriage. These photographs show that, although he's friendly, particularly to a pretty face, there was nothing untoward. The blonde woman you see is his cousin."

Mrs Porthaven's brow scrunched, and she stared at the photograph for a second. "I knew I recognised her. Miriam made a dreadful scene at our wedding. She drank too much champagne and fell over, landing in my great-uncle's lap. He almost had a heart attack when he realised what part of her he held."

I pressed my lips together so as not to smile. "That was unfortunate."

"When he recovered, he asked if he could come to our next gathering and have it happen again! I didn't know what to say."

"She was a lively sort," I said. "We had a conversation about pickled eggs."

Mrs Porthaven's eyebrows shot up. "You found nothing to enable me to end my marriage?"

"Not if you wish to sue on the grounds of unfaithfulness," I said. "But divorce is becoming less of a scandal. If you're unhappy, then move on. You're a woman of means and smart. Life without a husband has many benefits."

"I appreciate times are changing, but not for my family. You younger women have the freedom I can only dream of. You have no interest in past struggles." Mrs Porthaven sighed. "I am sorry. That was sharp. I find myself in a most unhappy predicament, and I'm stuck as to how to get out of it."

"A conversation with your husband may help," I said.

"That's not practical. There's only one thing to do. I have a home in France. I shall spend an extended amount of time there. They do say absence makes the heart grow fonder."

"Or makes one forget," I said.

"Indeed. I'll make the best of things. I appreciate you investing your time in this situation, and I trust you'll keep this matter within these walls." Mrs Porthaven stood and smoothed a hand over her skirt. "I cannot afford to be the source of any more gossip."

"We are the soul of discretion."

After saying goodbye and seeing her out, I returned to the office to find Jacob making a fresh pot of tea in our small kitchen.

"Another successful client meeting?" he asked.

"A client stoically resigned to the mistake of marrying a handsome face and discovering no substance behind it." I happily accepted a cup of tea.

"Two more enquiries came in while you were talking with Mrs Porthaven," Jacob said.

"That's good." My gaze went out the window, and I watched the passing foot traffic.

"Is something the matter?"

"No. Why do you ask?"

"Because you usually ask dozens of questions about any potential cases," Jacob said.

"My apologies." I hesitated then added, "I was thinking about the tunnels under the Green Man. We should go back this weekend and investigate."

"I'm uncertain that's a good idea." Jacob found a treat for Benji and fed it to him. "Despite Edmund's good intentions, he had no structural engineering skills. Those tunnels are a death trap."

"They looked safe enough," I said. "We should go. I enjoy keeping busy."

"Because it takes your mind off matters back home?"

"I regularly check in with my mother and Matthew. All is well there," I said. "And my mother is fostering two abandoned kittens. I know she'll complain about not getting enough sleep because of the bottle-feeding, but she's never happier than when looking after rescues."

Jacob was silent for several seconds as he sipped his tea. "I was referring to Ruby."

My gaze returned to the window, and I frowned as two prettily dressed women walked past, pushing prams. There were babies everywhere.

"You've barely mentioned her since you arrived," Jacob said. "The two of you did everything together until recently."

I'd revealed to Jacob that Ruby was hiding from me at Lady M's estate, but I had yet to reveal the reason for her deception.

"What am I expected to do? Ruby still wants me to think she's missing."

"She must think it odd you stopped looking for her," Jacob said.

"I wonder if any sensible thoughts pass through her head," I said. "She's got herself in a pickle and all because she wasn't thinking straight."

"Veronica, that's unkind," Jacob said. "And I've yet to learn of the specific pickle she's in. Perhaps I can assist."

"You can't. And it seems, neither can I."

Jacob stirred his tea. "Ruby is handling this mysterious muddle the best way she knows how."

"By pretending to go missing? And she's roped Lady M into the scandal, too, while excluding me. I could have helped. I would have fixed everything for her."

"By fix, do you mean taking over Ruby's life and forcing her to do things she doesn't want to do?" Jacob asked. "And before you protest and say you never force and that you're organised and efficient, you're known for being bull-headed. It's got you into a scrape or two in the past and will in the future."

I wrinkled my nose and then hunted in the cupboard for the packet of fruit shortcake biscuits I'd hidden for such an emergency.

"You know I'm right," Jacob said, as he took a biscuit from me.

"I wondered if Ruby was keeping a low profile because she feared my interference. But I'd only interfere to ensure the best for her," I said.

"You don't have to solve everyone's problems," Jacob said. "You have enough of your own."

"I have barely any problems. Just a busy schedule," I protested.

"Your mother telephoned three times yesterday to ask about you."

"Why didn't you say?"

"Because she asked me not to. She knew you'd worry."

"Is there something ailing her? Is it her heart? Perhaps I should go back to London—"

"This is why people don't tell you everything," Jacob said. "You're too quick to act."

"That is called efficiency."

Jacob arched an eyebrow. "I'm happy to share the load. We're partners in everything."

I reached over and squeezed his arm. "And I'm grateful for that."

"Don't be afraid to share what's worrying you," Jacob said.

"What do I have to worry about?"

"We've yet to reach a satisfactory conclusion about what to do with those photographs of your father. Is that what's got you so distracted?"

"I cannot think on that matter," I said. "I know you uncovered discrepancies in his death, but that's all it was. He's no longer alive. I've come to terms with that. And yes, those photographs of the man who looked alarmingly like him were shocking, but they can't be him. He'd never abandon his family."

Jacob opened his mouth to say more, but I shook my head and held up a hand.

"Give me time to feel comfortable opening the door on private, painful matters. I'm used to handling things alone. And while I appreciate having you in my life, that doesn't mean I'll change overnight."

Jacob's smile was rueful. "Overnight? We have been dating for months."

"I'm slow to change."

"You're stubborn."

"It's what you like about me."

His smile widened. "I like a woman who stands up for herself and to me."

"We can be stubborn together."

"Then may I stubbornly suggest you telephone Lady M and enquire about Ruby? She must think it awfully strange you've gone silent."

"Lady M lied to me, so I can no longer trust her. And if I telephone, I fear I may say something I regret if she continues to deceive me."

"That is your decision to make, but I've made my opinion clear," Jacob said.

"As have I. I'll finish this tea and walk Benji. The fresh air will do me good and give me time to think without my meddling partner influencing me."

"You adore my meddling almost as much as you adore Benji."

I couldn't hide my smile. Jacob was right.

I'd just finished my cup of tea when the telephone rang.

Jacob picked up the receiver. "One moment, please. It's for you. It's Lord Faversham's assistant. Felicity."

I drew in a sharp breath. I'd been waiting for this telephone call. I set down my cup and hurried over. "This is Veronica Vale."

"Miss Vale. Felicity Lorrimer. Lord Faversham has returned home earlier than planned. He wondered if you were free to meet this evening to discuss your proposal."

"I am at his disposal." I'd been courting Lord Benedict Faversham as part of my search for suitable grounds to expand the dogs' home into Kent. Lord Faversham had extensive grounds, and I'd happened upon an unused parcel of land when on a ramble with Benji. It had excellent stables that could be converted into a secure, warm shelter for dogs, and I'd wasted no time in discovering the owner and enacting my plan to conquer.

"Do you have a suitable office where you could meet?" Felicity asked.

"I have an office in Margate," I replied.

"That won't do. Lord Faversham won't want to travel after such a long journey today. Do you have somewhere local to Faversham?"

My temporary lodgings in the bed-and-breakfast wouldn't be suitable. "Would he be against visiting a local pub? I own the Green Man."

"Do you, now? I often stop in there for a gin and bitter lemon. They have a marvellous fireplace."

"It's a favourite feature of mine," I said. "And there's an office snug, which makes a suitable private meeting space. We could have dinner. We serve an excellent pie and mash."

"His Lordship is rather partial to a pie. I'm sure he'll be delighted to meet there," Felicity said. "Let's say seven o'clock?"

I happily agreed and, after setting down the telephone in its cradle, turned to Jacob with a huge smile.

"Good news?" Jacob asked.

"Lord Faversham is interested in supporting the expansion of the dogs' home," I said. "I'm meeting him this evening." I was already heading for the stairs, where I kept a small private space when I wanted no distractions.

"You focus on that," Jacob said, "and I'll come up and remind you when it's lunchtime. I know what you're like when you get engrossed in a project."

"Thank you. You're an angel," I said, my head already full of ideas on how to convince Lord Faversham to donate his land and stables to such a worthy cause.

Not every area of my life was smooth sailing, but I'd focus on the positives and ensure the unwanted dogs of Kent had the perfect haven.

---

I was ten minutes early to the Green Man, dressed in a smart, deep burgundy knee-length straight dress, though I'd kept my sturdy walking boots on since I planned to take Benji for a walk after meeting Lord Faversham.

As I entered the pub, I realised Lord Faversham was a better timekeeper than I was. I recognised him instantly. He was a tall man in his late fifties, with curly dark hair and a distinguished presence afforded by the obscenely wealthy. Sitting at his heels were his three gundogs. Black Labradors.

The dogs raced to greet Benji, surrounding him as they sniffed him from head to tail. Benji took it in his usual amiable stride, only giving a warning bark when one got a little too friendly.

Lord Faversham smiled when he saw me. "Veronica! I've already ordered you a gin fizz. I made it a large one because I expect we have plenty to talk about."

"Thank you. That's generous of you," I said.

"Think nothing of it." He reached down to pat one of his dogs. "You've been on my mind. I toured a few of my factories and saw all the unwanted animals. I understand times are hard for many, since the Great War took so much, but it chilled my heart to see so much suffering."

"It's a dreadful thing to witness."

He leaned back, watching me carefully. "I had your proposal with me and read it on my journey back. And I sent a man out to look around your place in Battersea."

"I trust the Battersea shelter lived up to your expectations."

"It's a marvellous place. So many volunteers, and all eager to help."

"That's how I got involved. Whenever possible, I volunteer."

"You must miss it, being down here."

"I do," I admitted.

"It's an excellent establishment. And perhaps one we can match here." Lord Faversham's voice held a note of optimism, and I felt a flicker of hope. "Do you have somewhere private where we could talk?"

"Absolutely. Follow me. We have a private snug." I acknowledged Colin, letting him know we'd take our dinner in half an hour, collected my drink, and led Lord Faversham and his pack of happy dogs away from the bustle of the bar.

As I pushed open the door, I was surprised to find the overhead light on.

Benji whined, making me slow. Then I caught the sharp, pungent tang in the air.

And that was when I saw Edmund's body on the floor.

# Chapter 4

"Good gracious! Whatever happened here?" Lord Faversham stood peering over my shoulder.

A faint groan surged me into action, and I raced to Edmund. He was alive, but barely. His skin was cold and clammy, and his breathing laboured. The amount of blood had convinced me he was dead.

"Stay still," I said. "Lord Faversham, call for help!"

After a second of dithering in the doorway, Lord Faversham dashed to the bar, hollering for assistance, leaving me in the room with a failing Edmund and Benji standing close by, softly whining.

"Is it just your head?" I asked. "Or are there other injuries?"

Edmund's hand fluttered against his chest as if attempting to reach into an inner jacket pocket.

"Don't move. Any exertion will be too strenuous," I said.

I adjusted my position, kneeling beside Edmund. Something crunched under my knee, but I was too busy checking for injuries to pay it much attention. Edmund kept fidgeting with his jacket, finally inching his fingers inside and pulling out a folded piece of paper.

"Help is on its way." Lord Faversham reappeared in the doorway. "Is there anything I can do for him?"

"I have basic knowledge of first aid, but a head injury this serious is beyond me." I didn't need to peer too closely at Edmund's head to realise he'd sustained a punishing blow. There was a worrying dent in his temple, and when I looked into his eyes, one pupil was dilated while the other remained wide.

"All we can do is keep him comfortable until help arrives," Lord Faversham said.

"Ask Colin for blankets," I said. "We keep a supply upstairs. Edmund will be cold because of the shock."

Lord Faversham was happy to take orders and remain occupied while I sat with Edmund. His breathing grew increasingly sporadic, his chest stuttering up and down.

"Don't give up on me," I commanded. "You have your family's stolen treasure to uncover. You can't do that from a hospital bed."

He pushed the piece of paper an inch towards me.

"You want me to look at this?" I asked.

Edmund didn't respond. I opened it to discover a hand-drawn map. It looked as though it corresponded to the tunnel system Edmund was investigating.

"Is this where you planned to take me when I joined you on our grand treasure-hunting adventure?" I hoped by keeping him talking, I would encourage him to keep breathing. "I won't be able to do this alone. And you won't want me getting my hands on all the treasure. I'll only donate the money to the dogs' home."

Edmund's eyes closed. His chest stopped moving.

"No, you don't! We'll have none of that. Come on now." I tapped him gently on his cheek.

"I have the blankets." Lord Faversham reappeared with a bundle in his arms.

I sat back on my heels and wiped an unexpected tear from my cheek. "I fear they'll be no use to him."

"Damn and blast it! I know the fellow. Come on, Edmund. What do you say to me bringing my business back to the bank? We always got on well, didn't we? That would secure you a hefty bonus. Take a breath, man."

Hurried footsteps approached the room, and Colin appeared along with a police officer carrying a litter. Two uniformed officers were behind him. I swiftly got out of the way, giving them a summary of what we'd discovered.

The policeman checked Edmund several times, listening for a pulse and examining the head wound. He stepped away from the body and shook his head. "There's nothing I can do. A head injury this severe... even if we'd been here when it happened, we wouldn't have been able to get him on the litter and to the hospital in time."

I was breathing too shallowly and felt light-headed, so I stepped back to compose myself. It wasn't the first time I'd happened upon a body, but this was a new experience, finding a chap taking his last breaths and being powerless to do anything. It felt so unfair.

Benji leaned against my leg for comfort, and I gently stroked his head.

"Would you like something to drink, Veronica?" Lord Faversham remained in the doorway, clutching the blankets, his face as pale as mine, no doubt.

"Something for the shock would be good," I said. "I'll be out in a moment."

"They're in the snug." I heard Colin's distant voice, and a few seconds later, relief and surprise flooded through me as Detective Geoffrey Bishop, Jacob's friend, arrived in the doorway.

"Ah, Veronica. I didn't expect to find you here," he said, by way of an introduction.

"Nor you," I said. "I didn't think your work stretched as far as Faversham."

"I move around, though I'm usually based in Margate." His gaze swept the room, a short wince crossing his face when he saw the body. "We're down on men, so we go where the work is. I was finishing a case at the local station when word came through about an injured man. Although no longer just injured. This is one of your pubs, I gather?"

I nodded. Geoffrey, Bishop to his friends, knew my history, since this wasn't our first meeting or our first murder.

"And you know the deceased gentleman?"

"Edmund Blackwood. He's been excavating the smuggling tunnels beneath the pub. He was following a family legend about treasure. Quite the local enthusiast. I agreed we could work on a project together. I thought it would be fun. I didn't realise he'd be here this evening, though."

"Thank you. I'll speak to you in more detail in a few minutes," Bishop said. "We need to check for evidence and assess injuries. I'll come and find you at the bar."

I looked around the room once more. There was no sign of any murder weapon. Two candlesticks sat on the mantel, and a fire iron rested on its stand, but they looked untouched. Since we'd stumbled in on Edmund not long after he'd received his injury, whoever did this wouldn't have had time to clean the murder weapon and put it back.

"Veronica, if you don't mind," Bishop said. "I know you have an interest in this area, but this is an official police investigation."

With a swift nod, I joined Lord Faversham, who stood in the corridor with his dogs.

"Let's get those drinks, shall we?" Lord Faversham asked.

"Good idea." The shock caught up with me, and I found my knees shaky, readily accepting Lord Faversham's arm as we walked away from the scene.

"There was nothing we could have done for him," Lord Faversham said after he'd placed the drinks order with Colin. "At least you were there in his last moments to comfort him."

"I hope I was some comfort," I murmured. "It's not my first brush with death, but it never gets easier."

"I expect you saw a few things during the war. Nursing, was it?"

"Something like that," I replied as I accepted the brandy he offered me.

"Terrible business. It leaves scars."

I nodded and sipped the drink, welcoming the warmth as it burned down my throat. "You said you knew Edmund?"

"I own several businesses, and the local ones banked with him. They're transport-focused, but I amalgamated their finances as we grew and moved our business away."

"What impression did you have of Edmund?" I asked.

"He was an excellent fellow. Conscientious, hard-working. As you said, he had a passion for exploring the less salubrious side of his family's history. We once got talking about the treasure he believed was hidden in the tunnels. I had a good laugh about it, but he was serious and said he planned on finding it."

I touched the map he'd given me, still tucked safely in my pocket. "I planned on doing some investigating myself."

"If there is any treasure, it would have been found a long time ago," Lord Faversham said. "Or destroyed. I know of at least a dozen smugglers' tunnels that have collapsed." His dogs danced around his heels, sensing the tension. "I'll return in a moment. These boys need an outside break. Unless you don't want to be on your own."

"I'm fine. Look after your dogs."

Bishop entered the bar from the snug. He looked around then walked over to me. "I've inspected the scene. It's unclear what happened, or rather, who walloped Edmund."

"It must have been someone who knows the pub layout," I said. "Customers aren't allowed into the snug. It's part of the private quarters. Colin has use of it. As do I."

Bishop already had his notepad out. "Colin is?"

"My landlord," I said. "He's worked here for years. A thoroughly reliable sort."

Bishop looked up as the main pub door opened. A brief smile crossed his face when he saw Jacob. Behind him, half a dozen police officers followed.

"What are you doing here?" I asked as Jacob approached.

"I was coming to surprise you," he said. "I wanted to see how your meeting with Lord Faversham went. Then I saw these fellows hurrying past and realised there was trouble."

"You could say that," I said, greeting him with a kiss on the cheek.

Jacob shook Bishop's hand. "Since you're here, I'm guessing it's serious?"

"Unfortunately, it is," Bishop said. "A man has been murdered."

"Edmund Blackwood. Struck on the head," I said. "I found him just before he passed."

Jacob looked momentarily startled. "Do we know who did it?"

"Not yet. But now more coppers are here, I'll have them speak to customers and find out who saw Edmund go into that room and if he was followed," Bishop said.

"Colin can help," I said. I called out for him, and a few seconds later, he appeared behind the bar, a cautious look on his face.

"How's Edmund doing?" he asked.

"He didn't make it," I said. "A terrible head injury did him in."

Colin puffed out a breath, his whiskered cheeks expanding. "I don't suppose he fell and hit his head on the corner of a table?"

"There's no evidence to suggest that," Bishop said. "Do you know what time Edmund arrived?"

Colin shook his head. "He snuck in without me noticing. I wouldn't have let him into the snug without getting permission."

"I agreed Edmund could use the snug, but I would have needed him to vacate when I arrived with Lord Faversham," I said.

At that moment, Lord Faversham returned with three much calmer dogs.

"Now you have support here, I'll leave you to it," Lord Faversham said, nodding at Bishop and Jacob. "You must have a lot to deal with."

"If you could give your details to one of my colleagues," Bishop said, "we will need to speak to you."

"Oh, of course. Anything I can do to help, just ask." Lord Faversham headed off with a police officer to provide his contact information.

I sighed. This was the opposite of how I'd expected the evening to go, but I couldn't think about my charity's needs, not when a man's body was cooling in my snug.

"You're sure you didn't see Edmund go into the snug this evening?" Bishop asked Colin.

"This is a popular pub. We always get the regulars in after work, and I'm shorthanded. I was covering everything, dealing with the bar while our cook was making our pie and mash for the evening. That always brings in extra people."

Bishop made a note on his pad, his attention distracted by the group of officers waiting for orders. "I'll be back in a moment." He gathered the men, conferred with them, and then they split off to talk to customers.

"What do you make of all this?" Jacob asked me as he accepted half an ale from Colin.

"Trouble," I said. "And in my establishment, that is unacceptable."

Bishop returned. "Someone will have seen Edmund enter the pub. Apparently, he's well known around here."

"He worked as the local bank manager and was often in here," Colin said. "You can get into the tunnels by going through the cellar. I wish I'd never agreed to let him in. The man was a nuisance. He was always bothering me."

Bishop's eyes narrowed. "He got in your way? Prevented you from working?"

Colin hesitated. "He could be a pest. Sometimes I'd send him away with a flea in his ear when he got belligerent. Some folk would think he owned the place."

"Why did you let him into the tunnels if he caused you trouble?" Bishop asked.

Colin glanced at me then ducked his head. "He paid me. Not a lot, but he said if I looked the other way and let him come and go, he'd make it worth my while. He preferred going into the tunnels this way because it meant he didn't have to walk onto the marsh when the weather was bad."

"Did something go wrong with the arrangement?" Bishop asked. "Edmund stopped paying?"

"No! It was easy money." Colin rubbed the back of his neck. "But I keep the cellar locked when I'm not going in and out for barrels or bottles of wine. And he'd show up and demand access. I had to leave the bar, get the key, and take him down there. Then we'd have to shift all the boxes so he could get into the tunnel. It was more trouble than it was worth."

"You could have changed your mind about the agreement," Bishop said.

"I thought Edmund would get bored," Colin admitted. "But he kept coming back. The man was obsessed with finding this imaginary treasure."

"He never found anything?" Jacob asked.

"A few rusty old bits of iron. Some coins. That's about it," Colin said.

"Yet he kept looking," Bishop mused. "Which suggests he thought he was close to uncovering the treasure. A treasure that would be worth a fortune to the finder."

"I know nothing about that," Colin said. "I kept out of his way."

"Did you leave the bar at any time this evening?" Bishop asked. "Check to see what Edmund was up to?"

"I must protest," I interjected. "Colin is an excellent fellow. I'd trust him to watch my back in any situation."

"We'll be asking everyone here the same question," Bishop replied.

"You're wasting your time thinking Colin had anything to do with this," I said.

"I appreciate that, Miss Vale," Colin said. "I was behind this bar all evening. Hard at work, just as I always am."

Bishop stared at him. "You didn't leave at any point?"

"Who would serve the drinks if I weren't here?" Colin asked. "You can ask any of the customers. Now, I need to get back to work. There are thirsty patrons, and they'll all be gossiping about what's going on."

"I may have more questions for you," Bishop said.

"And he'll answer them when he's able to," I said firmly. "Don't disrupt his business. Or mine."

"I may need to," Bishop replied. "Once we've spoken to everyone, we'll close the pub and make sure we haven't missed vital information."

I gritted my teeth but nodded. It would be an inconvenience to close the Green Man, but I understood why it had to be done.

Bishop headed off to gather information from customers, while I remained at the bar with Jacob and Benji. I glanced around the pub, studying people for signs of guilt, but all I saw were curious looks and excited glances. They kept peering towards the snug, hoping to glimpse Edmund's body being carried out.

"Veronica," Jacob muttered. "You have that look on your face."

"I believe it's called shock."

"Not that. It's an expression that makes me nervous," Jacob said. "Leave this matter to the police."

"Did I say I'd do anything else?"

Jacob cocked his head, much like Benji did when he suspected a hidden treat was about to be revealed.

I sighed. "Very well. A man was murdered in my pub. We must find out what happened."

# Chapter 5

"You should take to your bed to recover." My mother, Edith Vale, sounded positively faint on the other end of the telephone, her breathing rapid and tone shrill.

"There's no need for that," I said. "I had an excellent night's sleep. And this isn't my first body."

"Veronica! Don't talk like that," my mother said. "This is a nasty business. And in one of our pubs again! I'm beginning to think you attract trouble."

"I've had the same thought," I said. "But I assure you, Edmund's death had nothing to do with me."

"You invited him to the Green Man to use the snug!"

I was settled at a worn desk in the Green Man the morning after the murder, Benji by my side, enjoying a strong cup of coffee provided by Colin, and updating my anxious mother about my latest puzzle.

"He'd already made himself at home, thanks to Colin and his desire to earn a few extra coins," I said. "Edmund has been scouring the tunnels for a long time, hoping to find his family's fortune."

"What trouble has Veronica got herself into this time?" my brother, Matthew, called faintly in the background.

"Another murder," my mother said. "I should send you to Faversham to bring her back. She's not safe to be out on her own."

"Mother, don't you dare send Matthew anywhere. Unless it's to the bakery to get fresh bread and scones," I said. "I already have Jacob watching my every move. You know he doesn't enjoy me getting into scrapes and mischief."

"That man is lax with your freedom," my mother said. "He should have been by your side when you discovered that body."

"He's my companion, not my jailer," I said. "None of that talk! You know we have everything set how we like it. Jacob has his business, and I come and go as I please. It suits us. And he arrived shortly after I discovered Edmund, as did his friend, Detective Geoffrey Bishop. Thanks to him, I'll have an inside scoop on the situation."

"You worry me half to death with your snooping," my mother said. "Have you discovered any suspects?"

I didn't hide my smile, since my mother couldn't see my face. She professed to deplore my investigations, but she was always the first to dig for more details, and the gorier, the better.

"Not yet, but it's early days," I said. "The police instantly questioned Colin Winters. It wasn't him. Do you remember him? He looks like a grumpy pirate."

"I do, although not well," my mother said. "Your father took me down to Faversham several times. I remember the Green Man. There were tales of the smuggling tunnels and hidden treasure back then. It's all stuff and nonsense."

"You must have some idea of who's involved." Matthew's voice was clearer, so he must have settled on my mother's bed.

"I intend to ask around today, discover the lay of the land. Edmund worked as a bank manager, so he'll be well known."

"Perhaps he denied someone finance, and they got their revenge," Matthew said.

"Don't put ideas into your sister's head," my mother said.

"All ideas are welcome," I said. "And although Jacob isn't keen, I intend to find out what happened to Edmund. After all, the man died in our snug. It's only right I get to the bottom of matters."

"You'll tread on the policeman's toes and find yourself behind bars for interfering with things that don't concern you," my mother said. "Keep us up to date. I don't like to think of you getting into any trouble."

"Speaking of trouble, how's your new gentleman friend?" A change of topic to something that would fluster my mother should distract her thoughts away from me.

"What do you mean, trouble? Colonel Basil is an absolute gent," my mother said.

"He bought flowers," Matthew said, not sounding impressed. "Twice."

"How charming of him," I said. "Is he behaving?"

"Of course he's behaving!" My mother sounded indignant. "Nothing is unbecoming about our friendship. He's a man of a similar age to me, so we share stories. I'm glad of his company. It's not as if either of you spends time with me. What with Matthew training Felix in the garden and you gallivanting off to get yourself into troubling situations, I have to find amusement where I can."

"You absolute fibber," I said. "I know Matthew went out and bought you fish and chips two nights ago, and you ate them with him sitting at the bottom of your bed, the foster kittens between you. And he told me he got up in the night because you knocked over your glass of water and scared yourself and then read to you for an hour."

"That wasn't me! That was one of those pesky kittens. I don't know why you keep fostering them. They're such hard work."

"Which you have plenty of time to undertake," I said. If I didn't stimulate my mother with new fosters, she'd wither in that bed, consumed by her malaise and fear of a dreadful world that no longer existed.

"We had a telephone call from the dogs' home," Matthew said. "They've found a permanent home for the kittens, so they'll be gone soon. But they've had an intake of puppies."

"No puppies!" my mother exclaimed. "They chew everything. And as for the mess they leave around the house, the less said about that, the better."

"I'll take care of them," Matthew said. "It's not as if I've got anything else to do."

"You look after me. That's a full-time occupation," my mother said.

"You let Matthew enjoy himself," I scolded her.

Despite our bickering, we rubbed along fine together. My mother would always be anxious and fretful while Matthew and I were tolerant and compassionate, welcoming every moment we spent with her, realising there might not be many left. Well, barely a handful, if you believed what she said about her ailments.

"You must tidy this matter at the Green Man and come back swiftly," my mother said. "There's something waiting for you."

"What's that?" I asked.

"A letter. And from the handwriting, it's from Ruby. She has that messy scrawl. Her penmanship is as muddled as her mind."

"Oh. Why is she writing to me?" That small, hard ball of frustration I felt in the pit of my stomach whenever I considered Ruby's situation rolled around.

"I thought you'd be pleased!" my mother said. "You've been worried about her absence, and here we have a letter. It'll explain everything. I'll read it to you."

"There's no need," I said.

"I thought you'd want to know everything."

I bit back a sigh. "You've already opened it, haven't you?"

My mother shushed Matthew as he began to speak. "As if I'd do such a thing! Although... I may have inched it open by accident, thinking it was for me."

"Go ahead. Tell me Ruby's news." I'd be fascinated to hear what lies she was telling.

Rustling came down the telephone line, and my mother cleared her throat.

*Dearest Veronica, I hope you've not been missing me too much. I've been having a splendid adventure! I've been so busy that I haven't been able to tell anybody about it.*

"You see. She's right as rain, just as I knew she would be," my mother said.

"Indeed, it sounds as if she is," I said. "Does she give details of this splendid adventure?"

"I'm getting to that bit," my mother said. She continued reading.

*I'm sorry I've not been in touch, and I hope you haven't been too worried. I took a short trip up to Scotland and then extended my stay when I met a wonderful man who decided to show me the sights.*

I narrowed my eyes, my fingers flexing. Ruby was lying. She never lied to me. What did she think I'd do when I learned of her pregnancy? Or did she plan to hide from me for the rest of her life once she became a mother?

My gaze widened a fraction. Perhaps she intended to have the baby adopted. Would she do that? Was Ruby so concerned about my opinion that she'd hide her pregnancy and then abandon her child? My thoughts were too scattered to find any sense in this scrappy situation.

"Are you still there?" my mother asked. "You're usually full of questions."

"Perhaps I'm in shock. Ruby has been missing for some time."

"This is good news! As we suspected, Ruby has gone on an adventure and met a nice chap. I wonder if he wears a kilt."

"Not all men who live in Scotland wear kilts," Matthew said.

"What would you know about it? You've never been there," my mother countered.

"I served with several Scots during the war," Matthew said. "They used to joke about their sporrans."

My mother sniffed. "Let me continue the letter."

"Please don't," I said. "I've heard enough. We know where Ruby is and what she's up to. That's the main thing."

"But there's another page! Ruby talks about everything they've seen in Scotland."

"I don't want to know," I snapped. "Ruby's business is her affair. It has nothing to do with me."

My mother paused. "I don't understand. You can't be jealous of her going off and having an adventure on her own."

"Nothing Ruby does stirs any emotion in me." I closed my eyes and pressed a finger to my forehead, massaging away the headache threatening to take hold. "My apologies. I don't mean to be short with you, but I have a lot on my mind."

"You always have murder on your mind, and that's the problem," my mother said. "And it'll get worse now you have this business, snooping into misdeeds and shenanigans."

"If you're referring to my private investigation work, I'm happy to say it's flourishing. There's nothing wrong with assisting those who feel harm or injustice has been done to them."

"It's keeping you away from home, and that's unnatural," my mother said.

"Then perhaps we should end this conversation. The sooner I investigate what happened to Edmund, the sooner I'll be back in London, seeing to your every need."

"You never do that. Even when you're home, you're gallivanting about on newspaper business for your uncle."

"Do you mean undertaking tasks in my career to ensure I maintain my job as an obituary writer?"

"Matthew, I'm having one of my turns! Take the telephone," my mother declared.

A few seconds later, Matthew sighed heavily into the receiver. "It's not like you to be so snappy."

I exhaled. "I apologise again. I'm glad to hear Ruby is well, and I didn't mean to make Mother have one of her funny turns. Has she expired?"

"Don't joke. It's only because she misses you," Matthew said. "I'll go to the dogs' home and collect the foster puppies. They'll keep us so busy, she won't even think about you."

"That's quite a journey to undertake," I said. "Are you up to travelling all that distance?"

"I've been practising. I go out every day with Felix. I even spoke to a stranger on the corner. He had a dog, too."

I nodded in approval. Matthew had returned from the Great War a changed man, his experience leaving him with odd compulsions and a preference for staying indoors. He rarely left the house but was making a real effort, re-establishing a healthy routine. In large part, that was thanks to Felix, the rambunctious young dog we'd taken in as a foster. I considered him a foster fail, because Felix had never left, but he'd become an asset to Matthew.

"Matthew, I require my salts!" my mother's voice wailed in the background.

"I'd better go before she really does expire," he said. "Do you want me to send Ruby's letter to your office in Margate?"

I wrinkled my nose. "It can wait until my return."

"It's no trouble," Matthew said.

"It's more trouble than it's worth. Thank you. Now, keep an eye on Mother and make sure she doesn't perish under her bedsheets."

We said our goodbyes, and I set down the telephone. My fury and frustration refused to abate, despite Benji resting his head on my knee, offering the soft comfort of his fur as I absentmindedly stroked his ears.

"This will do no good," I muttered. It was time to channel these feelings into something productive.

I left the pub and walked outside to snatch some fresh air. It was early, but most of the local businesses were already setting up shop. I made my way along the front of the pub and turned into the passageway that led to a back door. It was a route used only by employees.

The door led into a corridor with a storeroom, a cupboard for cleaning supplies, and a small kitchen. If you continued along the corridor, you came to the snug where I'd found Edmund's body.

I paused as something crunched under my shoe. Crouching, I discovered a fine layer of sand. Benji sniffed it then turned and trotted back towards the street.

Frowning, I followed him, noticing more grains of sand scattered along the passage. Benji continued his pursuit, nose to the ground, sniffing intently as he padded forward.

A few moments later, he stopped, lifted his head, and glanced over his shoulder to check I was with him.

"What have you got?" I asked.

He resumed his sniffing, leading mc a few more paces.

The trail of sand was faint but distinct, running close to the buildings. It had yet to be disturbed by footfall, and with no recent rain, it remained intact.

Why would there be a trail of sand leading away from the pub? We followed it further, but then, abruptly, it stopped.

I walked back and forth several times, even crossing the road to see if the trail continued on the other side, but it was gone.

Returning to the back door of the pub, I stepped inside. Sure enough, more grains of sand dotted the corridor.

I checked the storeroom, the cleaning cupboard, and the kitchen, but there was nothing. Colin always ensured the place was spotlessly clean. I headed to the snug. There, nestled in the carpet, was more sand.

I frowned. My knee had crunched on something when I knelt beside Edmund as he took his last breaths.

"How curious," I murmured to myself. This wasn't a beach town, so it was unlikely anyone had simply tracked sand into the pub.

Benji and I stepped back outside, retracing our steps once more.

As I turned, movement caught my eye. A net curtain twitched on the other side of the road, stopping when they realised I'd caught them watching.

I marched across the street and rapped smartly on the black wooden door with its iron knocker. The house, as ancient as the pub, had a slight lean, dark beams running across the whitewashed exterior like the wrinkles of an old face.

No one answered.

I knocked again.

After a long pause, I heard faint shuffling from behind the door. Eventually, it creaked open, revealing a spry, tiny old lady. Her white hair was scraped back into a bun. She peered up at me with watery blue eyes.

"Good morning. I'm Veronica Vale," I said. "And this is Benji."

"Are you now?" the woman rasped, her voice scratchy with the telltale signs of someone who enjoyed a cigarillo or two.

"I own the pub across the road," I said. "Are you aware of what happened there recently?"

"I suppose you're talking about the murder?"

"Indeed I am." I studied her carefully. Intellect shone in her gaze. "Since you live so close, you may have seen something. Perhaps from your front window?"

The woman had kept her hands behind her back as we spoke, but with remarkable speed, she suddenly whipped out a gun.

# Chapter 6

I stared at the weapon. It looked antique, likely untouched for years. Even so, I instinctively shifted sideways, moving out of the direct line of fire.

The woman cackled. "I don't want to shoot you. But my joints are stiff. Help me clean and cock this, and I'd be happy to talk."

I eyed the gun. "Very well. I'd better come in. Mrs..."

"Florence Hatley," she said. "And it's Miss."

"Very well, Miss Hatley." I stepped inside the narrow hallway, and my jaw dropped.

My expression made Miss Hatley cackle again. "It's quite a sight, don't you think?"

I stepped forward and peered into a glass cabinet at a multi-headed tool with round balls at the end, spikes set into the balls.

"That's a flogging device." Miss Hatley shuffled behind me in her housecoat and slippers. "I have more on display if you want a tour."

I glanced at her. "And then we may talk?"

"So long as you shift the trigger on this thing, we'll talk."

"Then lead on."

I'd been wandering Miss Hatley's extraordinary home for almost two hours. Fascinating relics from the past were stuffed in every corner. It was like a mini museum, specialising in maritime exhibitions, with an interest in equipment used for punishment.

I stopped and tilted my head as a faint scratching reached my ears.

"It's not rodents, if that's what you're thinking," Miss Hatley said. "Napoleon is in the kitchen."

"And who might Napoleon be?" I asked.

"A Chihuahua. He's elderly, which makes him grumpy. I know that feeling," Miss Hatley said. "When you're old, everything aches, nothing wants to bend, and you can never remember what day of the week it is."

"If you're worried about Benji being unfriendly, you needn't be," I said. "He likes everybody, so long as they're kind to him."

"It's not your Benji I'm concerned about. Have you ever met a Chihuahua?"

"On many occasions," I replied. "I volunteer at a dogs' home in London. We get all manner of creatures left with us. They're often snappy because they're scared. Chihuahuas are always feisty."

"Napoleon lives up to that reputation. He may be small, but he's got the heart of a lion. And he's fearless. I don't want him nipping you."

"Benji will put him in his place if he oversteps," I said. "Let him loose. You can always hold him while we walk the rest of your collection. And I find dogs often follow Benji's lead in polite company. He's a well-mannered dog."

Miss Hatley eyed Benji, who wagged his tail at her. "Don't say I didn't warn you." She shuffled away, leaving me looking at an extraordinary collection of cudgels.

At first glance, I'd believed this to be a simple cottage with a two-up, two-down configuration. But Miss Hatley had an extensive cellar, which she'd packed with artefacts, and she planned on taking me into the loft, which she'd turned into an exhibit room.

"Here he is." Miss Hatley shuffled back into the room, a small, ragged-looking white Chihuahua tucked on her bony hip.

Napoleon growled the second he realised she had company.

"We'll have none of that." I reached into my pocket and pulled out several of Benji's favourite treats. I fed Benji two after he'd politely sat and waited then looked at Napoleon. His face was scrunched in a show of disgust that he was being ignored when food was on offer.

"You can have one," I said to him.

I received a growl in response.

"That's no way to speak to a lady," Miss Hatley said. "He's only used to me. We're too old to go out for walks, so we amble around the garden when we have a mind to. Sometimes, we go weeks without seeing people."

I fed Benji another treat, keeping a watch on Napoleon. It was clear he wanted a biscuit, but would he let his stubborn nature get the better of him and lose the opportunity to taste a delicious treat?

The growling turned into a sad whine. I tentatively reached out a hand and offered him a treat. He snapped at it, although he was aiming for my fingers, causing Miss Hatley to recoil.

We tried several more times, and eventually, Napoleon realised his growling and snapping, then his whining, would get him nothing.

"I should put him back in the kitchen," Miss Hatley said. "He's got no manners. I blame myself. I've overindulged him."

"We all overindulge our cherished dogs," I said. "Allow me to try one more time."

I spent a few seconds examining Napoleon's body language. His hackles had lowered, his tail was less stiff, and his nose twitched. The food was winning. I held out the treat, and while he was hasty when he grabbed, Napoleon didn't try to bite me.

He gulped down the biscuit, having a remarkably clean set of teeth for such an elderly dog, and then whined for more.

"Will you look at that?" Miss Hatley said in astonishment. "He never takes to anyone. Sometimes I wonder if he even likes me."

"I've been around dogs all my life," I said. "Most of their inappropriate behaviour comes from being misunderstood or having an ineffective owner. Although that's not you. It's clear you care for him."

Miss Hatley nodded. "I do my best."

"That's all any of us can do," I said.

"I'll take you to the loft, and you can look around. Then we'll stop for tea, unless you have somewhere to be," Miss Hatley said.

"I'm in no hurry," I replied, sensing Miss Hatley reccived few visitors and may appreciate the company.

The steps leading up to the loft were fixed in place, so it was easy to enter. The walls were lined with narrow shelves, guns on one side and various small, bulging sacks, some of which had handles or ropes attached to them, on the other.

"This is my gun collection," Miss Hatley said. "I've got behind in keeping them clean, but I was an expert shooter. I'd practise in the woods. Not hunting, just lining up tin cans and aiming at them. I should have joined the army. I'd have been a better shot than most of our poor young men who didn't make it home."

"What are the objects on this side?" I pointed at the sacks.

"When at sea, sailors must make do and mend. These are improvised cudgels." Miss Hatley gestured at the sacks. "The bags were filled with hard objects and then used to punish offenders."

I raised an eyebrow. "Goodness. What an unpleasant weapon."

"You must keep a smooth-running, obedient ship in the middle of the ocean," Miss Hatley said. "If there was a whiff of mutiny, things got out of hand. And sometimes the sailors could be uncooperative. Much like Napoleon." She nodded at the Chihuahua. "They get ideas and think they can run things if the captain isn't swift with the punishment."

I nodded as I inspected the brutal instruments. They were various shapes and sizes, many of them filled with compacted material or stones.

"Time for that tea," Miss Hatley said. "And while we're taking refreshments, you can help me cock that gun."

"About that..." I followed Miss Hatley downstairs. "What need do you have of such a weapon?"

"I have a shooting range in the back garden," Miss Hatley said. "I can't get to the woods anymore, but I don't want to lose my touch. You need to practise or your skills fade."

"As admirable as it is that you have such a skill, why do you need it?" I followed her into the tidy kitchen.

"We all need hobbies. If you don't keep learning, your mind grows dull." Miss Hatley bustled around, putting the kettle on the hob and setting out cups. "My body is decaying, but I don't want what's upstairs to go the same way. It's important to learn. It keeps the mind sharp."

"I couldn't agree more." I assisted with making the tea, since balancing Napoleon on one hip and undertaking the task was a struggle for Miss Hatley.

A few minutes later, we were settled in her cramped front parlour, tea in hand and a plate of digestive biscuits in front of us, the dogs eyeballing the plate.

"Is that why you observe the neighbourhood?" I asked. "It helps to keep your mind engaged?"

Miss Hatley chortled. "I'm nosy and bored. I like my neighbours, but they're busy. They work and don't have time for the old spinster who lives alone. It helps to pass the time to see what other people get up to."

"And your neighbours don't mind you shooting your gun in the garden?"

A laugh burst from her, ending in a raspy cough. "They can't stand it. It's why I keep an eye out to see when they go to work. I always get off several rounds before there are complaints."

"It's a shame you can't get to the woods," I said. "Napoleon would adore it."

"I used to walk there, but my knee has been bothering me," Miss Hatley said.

"Would you consider learning to drive?"

"My eyes won't permit that," Miss Hatley said. "I'm happy here. I have Napoleon, my shooting, and my collections. And, of course, my observations of the neighbourhood. It's enough to keep me occupied."

"Occupied enough to see any strange goings-on at the Green Man around the time of Edmund's murder?" I asked.

"I wish I could be of help." Miss Hatley set down her teacup. "I knew Edmund. He was a sensible man. I had little to do with him because I have no need to visit the bank for anything other than a simple cash withdrawal now and again. But everyone spoke kindly of him."

"Did you know he was interested in his family's history? Has he visited your collection?" I asked.

"He wouldn't waste his time coming here. I have nothing from his family in this house," Miss Hatley said.

"Did you know he was looking in the tunnels beneath the Green Man?" I asked. "He believed his family's treasures were still hidden there."

Miss Hatley gave an undignified snort. "We all have fancies we believe in, I suppose."

"You don't believe there's any treasure?"

"This town owes much of its fortune to the misdeeds of our ancestors," Miss Hatley said. "My family comes from a long line of seafarers, and they made their money on the waters. That's why I collect objects from their past. It was a different life, a different time."

"It sounds like you'd have liked to have been a part of that adventurous lifestyle," I said.

Miss Hatley's smile was wistful. "The Hatleys were one of the wealthiest families in this town."

"Do any of them still make their money from the sea?" I asked.

"Everything's gone. The respect, the fortune. Being a mariner is perilous," Miss Hatley said. "I wanted to go to sea, but I was told it wasn't a proper job for a lady. Although, nor is poking about in the business of murder."

"I'm happy to say times are changing," I said. "Although I've never heard of female mariners."

A wry grin wrinkled Miss Hatley's face. "I'm envious of your freedom. If I'd been born in a different time, I'd have made it my business to be on a ship, heading off to see what fortunes could be made."

"It does sound exciting," I said.

"Let me freshen our tea, and I'll tell you about my great-grandfather, Frank. Some of the treasures he brought back will astonish you."

"I'd like that very much," I said. "And leave Napoleon here. He's been eyeing Benji in a friendly manner. Perhaps the two of them would like to play together."

"If you're ready to risk it." Miss Hatley carefully set Napoleon on the floor. After a few seconds of tension, his little tail wagged, and he trotted to Benji so they could sniff noses.

Miss Hatley chuckled, shaking her head as she shuffled out of the room with the teapot in hand. As she left, Benji's tail smacked into a stack of paintings. Before they could topple, Miss Hatley lunged and grabbed them, setting them right.

"Nothing's broken, is it?" I asked.

"No harm done." She straightened up and waved a hand at me. "You sit right there. I'll be back in a few minutes."

I settled into the comfortable armchair, my gaze flicking over the extensive display of black-and-white photographs of various ships. I monitored Napoleon and Benji, but they seemed happy to sniff and wander as if they were the best of friends.

Napoleon marched to a corner where a stack of paper files rested. He tried to jump on them and sent them cascading to the floor. He yipped and ran away, barking a warning at Benji.

I stood to set the papers right. As I tidied the files, I discovered an old, yellowed diary. I didn't mean to read it since it was someone's personal business, but a few lines caught my eye.

*The Blackwood family must be stopped. They're ruining this business.*

*They've stolen our treasure, and they're pretending they know nothing about it. I will get it back. It's my family's name and reputation in tatters because of their lies, and I won't stand for it.*

I remained crouched on the floor, rereading the passage. My fingers brushed the front of the diary, and I looked at the inside cover. This had been written by Miss Hatley.

"What have you got there?" Miss Hatley stood in the doorway, the teapot in her hand and a scowl on her face.

"Napoleon knocked it over. I didn't mean to look, but..." I hesitated. "You sound angry about the Blackwood family."

Miss Hatley thumped the teapot onto the table and sighed as she returned to her chair.

I set the diary back in place and sat in my seat, glancing around to ensure Miss Hatley's gun was nowhere near her.

"It's ancient history," she said. "The Blackwood family treated mine poorly. We were both seafaring families, but they spread rumours about how we did business. We lost money, customers, and there were whispers that they stole a container from our shipments."

"A container full of treasure?" I asked.

"I'll never know for sure because no one talked about it. But they ruined everything."

"Does that mean you're glad Edmund Blackwood is dead?"

Miss Hatley's expression hardened. "He changed his family's course when he went into banking, but the smear of the past lingers. I wasn't sad to learn of his death. That's what he gets for poking around in the past and trying to find things that don't belong to him."

I gripped the edge of my seat. "Would you mind if I asked where you were on the night of his death?"

Miss Hatley startled in her seat. "You can't imagine I had anything to do with that."

"Were you home?"

"I've already told you I can't get out and about. I have a woman who brings my evening meals. I had my dinner, same as always, and then settled in to listen to the wireless and knit. That's as adventurous as it gets around here."

"You didn't go outside and see Edmund entering the pub?"

She folded her arms. "If you're done snooping and pointing the finger, thinking I had anything to do with that young man's death, it's time for you to go. Napoleon, show our guests out."

Napoleon looked confused at the order and danced around Benji, wanting to play.

"What about your gun?" I asked. "We haven't worked on it yet."

"I don't need help from you." Her voice was sharp. "You be on your way and stop interfering in things that don't concern you. You can see yourself out."

I stood and called Benji. We left the house, stepping into the bright morning. I squinted, momentarily disoriented after being inside the cramped, dim cottage for so long.

Miss Hatley played the part of a weak old lady perfectly, but she'd been quick when Benji knocked over those paintings. Was the frail spinster routine an act? Could Miss Hatley be hiding a murderous heart full of revenge for slights against her ancestors?

# Chapter 7

"We've had a request to investigate another adultery." Jacob sat opposite me at a round wooden table in the Green Man later that day.

Although the pub was yet to reopen to the public, we'd been allowed in since the police had finished their investigations. We'd be able to open tomorrow to regulars.

"I hope those aren't the only cases our agency becomes known for." I smiled at Colin as he brought plates of battered cod and chips. "It would get rather dull following around wayward men all the time."

Colin stifled a laugh as he caught the tail end of the conversation. "You ordered three plates. Do you not need the third?"

"Bishop has just arrived." Jacob nodded as Bishop dashed into the bar, looked around, spotted us, and hurried over.

"Sorry, I got caught up at the station. There's not enough of us to go around and far too much crime."

"I'll bring your lunch out, sir." Colin hurried away and returned a few seconds later with another plate.

Bishop ordered an ale, and we all tucked in.

"We'll keep a well-balanced portfolio of work," Jacob said to me. "There's more to life than chasing cheaters."

"What about that fraud case you were looking into?" I salted my chips. "That sounded interesting."

"It's still a possibility. But it's too early for us to get involved," Jacob replied.

"Just so long as you keep your noses out of murder," Bishop said.

"Ah. About that. Do you have any updates on what happened to Edmund?" I asked.

Bishop shrugged. "I can tell you little, because it's an active investigation, but we know from talking to patrons and neighbours that he was well-liked. Edmund came from a good family, although some people say they were eccentric due to their obsession over hidden treasure."

"Which was the reason Edmund was here," I said. "He was convinced his family hid a hoard of gold and gems somewhere in the old smuggling tunnels. I was indulging him by letting him use the snug as a base. I thought nothing serious would come of it."

"I don't expect Edmund thought his investigations would lead to such a sticky end," Bishop said. "Although, if you go back far enough in his family history, there's a chequered past. They made their money off the misfortune of others. Took what didn't belong to them and sold it. That's how they became so wealthy."

"I had a fascinating conversation with one of the pub's neighbours, Florence Hatley. She lives just across the way. I was retracing the killer's steps, and I noticed her watching and thought she might have useful information."

"How do you know which way the killer went when they left the pub?" Bishop asked.

"Benji discovered a fine trail of sand leading out of the snug and onto the road. We followed it, but then it disappeared."

"How is sand connected to the killer?" Jacob asked.

"That's what we were trying to determine. It was odd. Out of place."

"It may have nothing to do with what happened to Edmund," Bishop said. "Perhaps, when the pub was being cleaned, it got spilt out of a container."

"I can't figure out why there'd be sand in the pub in the first place," I said. "But getting back to Miss Hatley, she has a fascination with history, too. And there's a connection between Edmund's family and hers. An unhappy one."

"What did you learn?" Jacob asked.

"Although Miss Hatley told me she liked Edmund, when I pressed for more information, after discovering a worrying diary entry, she admitted she was glad he was dead."

"Should you have snooped around an innocent old lady's private belongings?" Bishop asked.

"You'll have to blame Napoleon for that," I said.

Bishop looked puzzled.

I carried on, "Napoleon is Miss Hatley's dog. He knocked over a pile of papers, and as I was putting them right, I saw a diary entry. It showed Miss Hatley's true feelings about Edmund's ancestors. They discredited her family and stole from them. Edmund's family became the most affluent in town, while the Hatley family was left to mockery and ruin."

"What are you suggesting, Veronica?" Jacob asked.

"Miss Hatley is sprightly for a mature woman, and she lives opposite the pub," I said. "It would have been a simple matter for her to enter the pub and deal with Edmund."

"Deal with him?" Bishop echoed, shaking his head with a smile. "I spoke to Miss Hatley. We knocked on all the neighbours' doors to learn if they'd seen anything useful. She's a scrap of a thing. A strong gust would knock her over, and she barely leaves the house. I can't imagine a less likely killer."

"I thought the same at first," I admitted. "But she professed to certain skills, and she was quick on her feet when Benji knocked over some framed photographs. It made me wonder if the little old lady act was just that to ensure no one suspects her."

"She's no threat," Bishop said.

"Miss Hatley lives alone. She had no company the night Edmund was murdered, other than the lady who brings in her meals. She had ample opportunity to get into the pub and commit the crime."

"We have more credible suspects." Bishop raised a hand as I began to protest. "And I know of her interest in collecting memorabilia, including weapons. She came to the door with a gun slung over her arm."

"Miss Hatley has numerous weapons that could have rendered Edmund unconscious," I said.

"But Edmund was knocked on the head. Such an assault is beyond a frail old lady," Bishop said. "I mean no disrespect to Miss Hatley, but she doesn't have the strength to commit such a deed."

"You shouldn't discount her," I said. "Perhaps she wasn't working alone."

Bishop set down his fork. "Be careful poking about in this investigation. I know you have experience, but you don't want to find yourself on the wrong side of the local police. I've no problem with what you do, but many won't appreciate your interference. Not all of us enjoy working with private investigators."

"The murder happened in Veronica's pub, so it's only right she's interested," Jacob said.

"And you are both welcome to updates," Bishop said. "But don't tread on too many toes. You won't find the policemen around here as tolerant as they are in London."

I laughed. "When I first met Jacob, he was barely tolerant of me being in the same room as him. He snapped and snarled and told me I was getting in his way. He even does that now, occasionally."

"I do not," Jacob grumbled. "Well, only when you steal the newspaper before I've had an opportunity to peruse it."

"Florence Hatley is of no interest to us," Bishop said, steering us back to the case. "But we are interested in Edmund's brother, Charles Blackwood. He's found himself in a spot of bother more than once and spent several nights in the police cells, usually sleeping it off after having too much to drink."

"Why is he a suspect?" I asked.

"Charles is the family's black sheep due to his liking for gambling halls. He's on his uppers. We've yet to track him down, though, given he's been kicked out of his last known address for not paying his rent. It won't surprise me if we find him sleeping on a park bench somewhere."

"Was he not close to Edmund?" I asked.

"From what we've discovered, Charles embarrassed Edmund. Edmund had made a respectable name for himself, and Charles was a disruption he didn't need, especially not one threatening his reputation."

"There was trouble between the brothers?" Jacob said.

"When we find Charles, we'll speak to him and discover just how deep that trouble ran," Bishop said. "For now, he's in the wind, and that makes him my number one suspect."

"He could have asked Edmund for money, especially if he thought he'd discovered the lost family fortune. It's a motive," I said. "If Charles is desperate for money, he could have pressed Edmund for a handout. If not from his savings, then from the family fortune."

"Or even from the bank," Jacob said. "Edmund must have earned a reasonable wage."

"He did, and his finances are in order," Bishop said. "He's got a respectable amount saved."

"If Charles hasn't been staying in Faversham, how would he know Edmund was using the pub's snug as his base of operations for treasure hunting?" I asked. "I only just gave him permission to do so."

"Perhaps Charles is only missing to us," Bishop said. "He could still be in the area. Men with a fondness for the gambling halls and a dislike for paying bills keep a low profile around law enforcement. For all we know, he could have been meeting with his brother regularly. But we won't know anything for certain until we find him."

"Since we're suggesting other suspects, what about May Shaw?" I asked.

"I don't know that name," Bishop said. "How is she connected to Edmund?"

"We met her here," I replied. "Edmund was extolling his excitement about the treasure and asking if he could use the smuggling tunnels. May overheard our conversation and was sly about Edmund's amateur approach. She's a local historian, and by all accounts, something of an expert."

"Did they have a disagreement when you were here?" Bishop asked.

"Not as such, but May was sharp with him. She put him in his place, and I don't think Edmund appreciated it."

"Thanks for the tip." Bishop took out his notepad and scribbled her name. "I'll look into it, but we're starting with Edmund's family then speaking to the bank employees."

"Excellent. You do that, and I'll tackle May," I said.

"Perhaps Bishop doesn't need our help," Jacob murmured.

"Fear not. I wasn't volunteering you for the role," I said with a smile. "You've got those adultery cases to look into."

Bishop chuckled as he tucked away his notepad. "You didn't hear it from me, but I appreciate the support, so long as you're discreet. We're being run ragged. I'm reporting to my boss back in Margate and then hotfooting it over here to help with this investigation. If you find any leads, pass them to me. The sooner we get this case cleared up, the better. Then I can go back to regular hours and a decent amount of shut-eye."

"I'll finish here and head out to locate May. I'll report back my findings." And perhaps winkle out a few clues. After all, I'd be assisting the overburdened police. It was my civic duty.

Jacob shook his head but smiled good-naturedly. He knew I was never happier than when hunting for clues.

After finishing lunch and feeding Benji a hearty plate of fish scraps and chips, we headed outside into the pleasant early afternoon sunshine.

The best place to search for information on May was the library. Since May was interested in history, it made sense she spent time there. Benji stuck with Colin, since libraries rarely welcomed animals.

Faversham library was an attractive building with weathered limestone trim, tall arched windows, and crowned with an ornate pediment above its heavy oak doors. When I entered, I was pleased to see it bustling with activity. After enquiring with a white-haired woman behind the front desk, I discovered May had a spot at the local archive, just down the road from the library.

I walked back outside and, a moment later, found myself in front of a beautiful old building with a delightfully crooked chimney stack. I entered and took a moment to enjoy the lovely surroundings before approaching a desk, where a mature gentleman wearing a pair of round spectacles looked up.

"Good afternoon. I'm looking for May Shaw. I believe she works in the archive," I said.

"Do you have an appointment?"

"No, but I'm hoping she's available." I introduced myself and let him know I was interested in speaking to May about the Blackwood family.

He made a brief telephone call then returned with a small smile. "Miss Shaw is in a meeting, but she won't be long."

"I'm happy to wait," I said. "Perhaps I could browse the archives?"

"Of course. I'll give you a visitor's badge and sign you in. We're proud of our archive and always welcome visitors."

"I can see why."

Five minutes later, I strolled among the beautiful stacks, inhaling the delicious scent of old paper as I brushed my fingers along the spines of books. Their topics ranged from crop rotation to dressmaking. It was a treasure trove of knowledge and history just waiting to be uncovered.

I discovered the section devoted to local residents and uncovered a wealth of information on the Blackwood family. Not knowing how long May would be, I took a book and settled in a chair to read.

Half an hour later, I was fully versed on their scandalous behaviour. There was talk of skulduggery and misdeeds, even highway robbery, and the capture of a vast ship at sea containing a small fortune in saffron.

I looked up as footsteps approached and smiled when I saw May.

"Miss Vale! This is a pleasant surprise," she said. "My apologies for keeping you waiting. I believe you want to talk about the old families of Faversham? That's always a treat for me."

"I thought it would be. Thank you for taking the time to see me." I returned the book to its shelf and smoothed down my skirt.

"I was intrigued when I received the message you were here," she said, gesturing for me to follow her. "Do you have time for a spot of tea?"

I nodded. "Absolutely. Tea and murder always make excellent companions."

# Chapter 8

"Murder, you say? Gosh. You must mean Edmund." May looked a trifle stunned when I mentioned murder but quickly recovered herself.

"I'm curious about what happened to him," I said. "Since his death occurred in my pub, you can understand why."

May was silent for several seconds then nodded. "I would be the same if I found a fellow no longer breathing in the archive. It's not mine, as such, but I spend so much time here that I think of it as my second home. I even have a key, so I can get in at all hours when inspiration strikes and I need to research a subject."

"I'm glad you understand."

"Follow me. This conversation requires something a little stiffer than tea." She marched away, leaving me with no choice but to follow her.

We walked past the beautiful book stacks into the main corridor, hurrying along until May stopped by a door and unlocked it.

"This is one of the few perks I have from being a long-standing member of the local Historical Society. After you've been a member for twenty years, you get access to one of the three offices they keep for visiting lecturers. I laid claim to this space, and I've scared away anyone ever since. It's my haven."

I stepped inside. It was an organised office space full of books and papers. There was a faint aroma of coffee in the air.

"Let me arrange the tea," May said. "And I keep a bottle of sherry in the bottom cupboard on the left-hand side, along with some glasses. You sort that, and I'll be right back."

May left me in the office, and I poured the sherry before glancing along her immaculately ordered bookshelf. Every book focused on the history of Faversham and the different maritime families known to the area.

"Here we are," May said as she returned. "I absconded with a visiting speaker's tea order, since I didn't want to keep you waiting." She set the tea tray down with a clatter before striding around the desk and settling into an old, worn, well-loved leather chair.

"I must confess to feeling a touch of envy at such beautiful surroundings," I said. "I often visit the archive in London."

"Oh, that must be magnificent," May replied. "London has all the facilities. Although I find it a touch busy for my taste. Saying that, Faversham is growing by the hour, it would seem. One day I expect it'll be as sprawling as London."

"I hope it never loses its charm," I said. "London is so vast that you only feel at home if you choose a particular part to call your own and become familiar with all the nooks and crannies."

May poured the strong tea into two china teacups. "That sounds like a sensible plan. So, you want to talk about Edmund?"

I liked a woman who got straight to the point. I settled in a chair with my teacup and sherry in front of me.

"I couldn't help but notice, but you didn't appear to think highly of Edmund," I said. "You were sharp with him when you met in the Green Man."

"That was hardly me being sharp. I'm honest. Sometimes, a little blunt for my own good. If a man behaved the same way, he'd be told he was forthright and sensible. But because I'm female..."

"I confess to being told I have a sharp tongue a time or two. It's got me in a spot of bother."

A smile played across May's lips. "Then we're cut from the same cloth. A cloth I highly admire."

"Then I'll come to the crux of the matter, since we're of similar minds. What was your relationship with Edmund?" I asked.

May sipped her sherry and leaned back in the leather chair. "I had a distaste for his treasure hunting obsession. It was childish. It made a mockery of history. He should have studied and gained a doctorate. Something I've longed to do since I was a young girl. But the opportunity was never there. Edmund had everything laid out before him, but he followed fancies and old whispers of nonsense. It was a wasted opportunity. That annoyed me."

"I see how it would," I said. "But at least you're following your ambitions now."

"I'm uncertain what the universities will think of an older woman applying for a Bachelor of Arts in History. But I refuse to give up. This has always been my passion."

"And it appears it was Edmund's," I said.

May hesitated. "Yes. We had that in common, although we went about things differently. Few people in this town are as passionate about the past as I am, but he was one of them. I am sorry he's dead. The man was a nuisance, but he wasn't malicious. He even came to my talks."

"You give presentations?"

"On the history of smuggling in the town, among other things," May said. "Edmund would attend my lectures and often asked intelligent questions. Sometimes they veered into his fanciful beliefs about treasure, but he knew his stuff."

"Did he ever get in the way of your work?" I asked.

"Not as such. Although several chaps suggested Edmund should take on this role. The nerve!"

"Your position here is full-time?"

"It is. Although I had to fight for that," May said. "After the war, as I'm sure you know, many men returned and wanted to take the positions they'd left when they served their country to protect us all."

"You almost lost your job?" I asked.

"After the war, the board of trustees considered having a man take over the position. They interviewed several candidates, and I insisted on being included on that list. I knew I could beat any of them. I've visited this archive since I was fourteen and worked my way from the bottom. I used to be the tea girl! I know the place inside and out."

"I'm glad you fought for your place," I said. "I had a similar situation. My work at the London Times as their obituary writer has involved more than a few heated conversations with the men in the office about how journalism is no place for a woman."

May tutted. "It's an outdated view. We're more than capable. We proved that during the Great War. And yet we're expected to stay at home, stand in front of the cooker, and be grateful."

Although this was a pleasing diversion in the conversation, it was time to steer May back to the topic at hand. "I'm sure you've already been asked, but where were you on the night of Edmund's death?"

May stared at me levelly then drained her glass before refilling it. I'd barely touched mine, and she didn't offer me more.

"You consider me involved in this unsavoury matter?" she asked.

"You've been open about being frustrated by Edmund's actions," I said. "You can't be surprised that you're considered a suspect."

"I am! And I'm unhappy to be accused," May said, her tone clipped. "What credentials do you have to question me in such a manner? You just told me you work for a newspaper."

"I have more than one talent in my armoury," I said. "And I have an alarming ability to stumble into many a murderous situation. Partly because of my curious nature, but more recently, I've opened a private investigation agency in Margate."

May raised a brow. "Private investigation? Goodness, that's a turn-up for the books. You said us. Do you work with a companion?"

"Yes. A former policeman from London, Jacob Templeton. We went into business together, and it's going well. That work has evolved my ability to unravel puzzles."

"And the puzzle you want solved is what happened to Edmund in your snug?"

"Naturally. Which is why I'd appreciate your cooperation."

May pressed her lips together before nodding. "You're doing a more thorough job than the police. I was here. As I've mentioned, I have a key, so I can come and go as I please. On the evening of Edmund's murder, I was ensconced in a fascinating manuscript about tunnel excavation."

"Were you alone?"

"The archive officially closes at five o'clock, so there would have been no one else here," May replied. "I suppose someone might have seen me entering or leaving, but you'd have to check with the local businesses."

"What time did you leave?"

"When my eyes were so tired, I could barely see. It must have been around ten o'clock that evening." She paused, then added, "I will admit to finding Edmund akin to a burdensome fly at a glorious picnic. I'd swat him away when he became too irritating. But I had no desire to end the man's life. We had different approaches to the same topic, but I bore him no serious grievance."

It was clear May was an intelligent woman with a firm set of ideas. Would she have stooped to the business of murder? She thought little of Edmund, certainly, but I felt no malice from her towards him.

She must have sensed my internal dilemma. "I wouldn't ruin a promising future by committing murder. It's illogical. And I'm proud to be a woman who favours logic over feelings."

"Then we have more than one thing in common." I raised my sherry glass.

We finished our tea and sherry with more convivial conversation, and I left the archive and returned to the Green Man to collect Benji, my head full of questions.

Colin was behind the bar, shelving clean glasses, when I entered. He greeted me with a smile. "Are you still working on the case?"

"Indeed, I am. And I'll continue to do so until this mystery is solved," I said. "Have you had any more bother from the police?"

"They're leaving me alone," Colin said. "And I'm glad of it. I don't need trouble coming to my door."

"You had nothing to do with this," I said as I received a warm greeting from Benji. "I wanted to ask you about May Shaw. She confessed that she had no fondness for Edmund."

"I should say she didn't," Colin said. "They were always arguing. It sometimes got nasty."

"In what way?" I asked.

Colin reached across the bar and tossed Benji a large piece of pork scratching, which he grabbed with a happy woof.

"They were always bickering over their families or the tunnels and how unfair it was that Edmund got his foot in the door before May could."

"May was interested in investigating the tunnels, too?" I asked.

"Of course. Why wouldn't she? You'd be set for several lifetimes if you uncovered that mythical treasure they go on about."

"I didn't think May was interested in the treasure, more about preserving historical accuracy."

Colin snorted. "Historical accuracy won't put food on the table. She even tried to have me ban Edmund from the pub and the tunnels. She said he cheapened history, and I should be ashamed of myself for letting him anywhere near such precious materials."

"But Edmund twisted your arm by slipping you money." I arched an eyebrow.

Colin had the decency to blush. "That wasn't my proudest moment. If I hadn't let him get so involved, he'd still be alive."

"You're a good man, and Edmund's death has nothing to do with you," I said.

"I wouldn't be surprised if May whacked him on the head," Colin said. "There's been an ongoing rumour that her family fled to Australia after dubious dealings with the Blackwoods."

"Gosh. What kind of dealings?" I asked.

"I don't know the ins and outs, but I imagine the Blackwoods destroyed the Shaw family reputation. They were known for it. It's no secret."

I leaned against the bar. "It would appear the Blackwoods enjoyed ruining any family of note."

"Some people hate competition." Colin finished polishing a glass. "What plans do you have for the rest of the day?"

"If you'd be so good as to pour me a swift coffee, then I must return to my research," I said. "People around here are keeping too many secrets for my liking, but I intend to find out what they are and if they relate to Edmund's murder."

# Chapter 9

The next morning, I enjoyed a peaceful breakfast with Benji's charming company. He was being exceptionally delightful because my landlady, Jenny, had provided me with a splendid spread. Warm crumpets, a rack of toast, kippers, and poached eggs. It was an eclectic selection but ensured I'd not need to stop for food during what promised to be a busy day.

I fed Benji a small piece of toast and a slice of kipper. He'd already had breakfast, but there was always room for an extra treat.

Jenny bustled in with a brown teapot in hand and freshened my cup without even asking.

"Do join me," I said.

"Don't mind if I do." Jenny was a thin lady in her early fifties. She never remained still for long, and if she wasn't darting about, her eyes were ever watchful, always looking for something to tidy. "I've been on my feet since dawn. The couple in room five left a mess. Still, they were young and honeymooning, so I can't blame them for not being too tidy. They had other things on their minds."

"They should have made time to ensure there wasn't too much work for you," I said.

"I like to keep busy." Jenny smoothed a hand over the tablecloth. "What adventures await you today?"

When I'd booked my room in Jenny's quaint bed-and-breakfast, I'd informed her of my occupation as a private investigator. She'd been fascinated and grilled me about the type of work I did and whether I found resistance to having such an unusual occupation as a woman.

"I'm still investigating the terrible business at the Green Man," I said.

"That's a pleasant pub," Jenny said. "It's a tragedy such a thing happened there. Well, it would be a tragedy if it happened anywhere."

"It remains a mystery as to what happened to Edmund Blackwood," I said.

"I've been talking to my friends at the bakery. It's all they're interested in."

"Do they have any suggestions as to who may have harmed Edmund?"

"They keep talking about his brother. I suppose you know about him?"

"Charles Blackwood," I said. "Yes, he has come to the police's attention. Have you ever met the man?"

"Unfortunately, I have. He's a troublemaker. It's such a shame, since he was once a respectable gent, much like the late Mr Blackwood. He'd walk around in a suit and tie, with his shoes polished and his hair neat. But you should see him now. A scruffy beard, filthy clothing, and he enjoys a drink. And don't get me started on the gambling." Jenny tutted.

"I heard Charles got himself in trouble in a gambling hall," I said. "The police would like to speak to him. He may not even know his brother is dead."

"You would think a curse follows that family," Jenny said. "They always find themselves in bother. They used to be well-respected, but then people learned how they came about their fortune, and that sort of tarnish sticks. Ever since then, bad luck has followed them."

"What kind of bad luck?" I asked.

"Well, Mr Blackwood being murdered is the worst sort of luck you'd want finding you," Jenny said. "But I remember a grandfather running into trouble with a house he bought. A problem with the deeds meant he spent a fortune in the courts, ensuring his house wasn't seized. And there was another man, an uncle. He found himself in trouble for not paying his taxes. He said he had, but there were no records of the payments. He ended up spending time in prison. I believe he died behind bars."

"I've been reading about the Blackwood family," I said. "Their fortune came from crooked means."

"Smuggling and stealing. We can be plain about that," Jenny said. "Mind you, they weren't the first family who made their wealth in such a way. Not that it happens much anymore. Well, I suppose one or two things slip through unnoticed, but just about every other family smuggled something along the tidal creek and through this town."

"Yet not all of them were cursed like the Blackwoods," I murmured, more to myself than to Jenny.

"That family must have upset someone important," Jenny said.

"Did you ever see Charles and Edmund disagree over anything?" I asked.

"There were fights, but I wouldn't say they disliked each other," Jenny said. "It was typical brother behaviour. Siblings are like that. They argue one minute, make up the next. Although in this case, it was usually when Edmund paid Charles's debts. That poor fellow has no money, but he can't stay away from the gambling halls."

"Are the halls you refer to in Faversham?" I asked.

"We have three in town that I know of. All of them run by unpleasant characters."

"Charles needs to know what happened to Edmund," I said. "And the police have failed to locate him."

"And you want to?" Jenny shook her head. "You'll find yourself in hot water if you poke around those venues. Not everyone follows a godly way of living. The men who run those places cheat, lie, and steal to get what they want. And they're not above hurting ladies."

"I'm always careful," I said. "And I have Benji by my side. He protects me."

Jenny smiled fondly at Benji. "I can see he adores you. No doubt because you fed him half your kipper."

"He had a small piece, and he told me it was excellent."

Jenny chuckled good-naturedly.

"Could you provide me with the addresses of these gambling houses?" I asked.

"You shouldn't go there. It's not safe." Jenny's expression grew worried. "Leave that to the police."

"The problem is the people who run these establishments will never talk to the police. They see a uniform and go silent. They won't see a woman alone as any threat."

"At least take a chaperone," Jenny said. "I'd offer to come with you, but I've got too much to do here."

"That's kind of you, but the addresses will be enough," I said. "And I know how to look after myself."

"I imagine you do, running your own agency," Jenny said. "Give me a moment. I'll note down the details. But I want to see you back here this evening to give me a full account. I won't sleep if I know you've got yourself in trouble."

Ten minutes later, after polishing off my breakfast, collecting the addresses from Jenny, and receiving yet more warnings to take care, we headed away from the residential area and walked along a surprisingly busy road, given how early it was. The houses grew smaller and grimier, and it was soon clear we were in the less salubrious part of Faversham.

I double-checked the details Jenny had given me and identified a small green door she'd told me to look out for. It was alleged to be a business establishment called *McGuire and Company*. Jenny assured me it was a front for a gambling house, even though they pretended to supply loans to small businesses.

I knocked on the door but got no answer. Just as I was considering searching for a back entrance, a door opened in a house on the opposite side of the road, and two rough-looking chaps stumbled out, blinking in the sunlight like startled moles. Their clothing was creased, they had straggly beards, and one of them was missing a shoe.

After watching them go, I crossed the road. The building was a hostel for retired or disabled merchant seamen. This was the perfect place for a man down on his luck to hide.

I entered the hostel and paused, uncertain which way to go, as I reached a small lobby area with numerous doors.

A door opened, and a tired-looking, middle-aged man peered out. A smile creased the corners of his eyes. "You must be Gladys, from St. Saviour's church. I was beginning to think I'd have to serve the breakfasts on my own."

I hesitated. Pretending to be Gladys would get me into the hostel. "I'm happy to help with serving breakfast."

"Oh, thank goodness for that. I'm Harold."

"It's a pleasure to meet you."

He nodded towards Benji. "Does he behave? We don't usually allow animals, although some of the men have dogs they keep as friends."

"He's exceptionally well-behaved," I said. "Benji will sit by the kitchen door so as not to cause trouble while we serve."

"Hurry then. There have already been grumbles because I burned the toast. I'm not used to doing this, but with everyone off sick with that stomach problem, I have no option but to get stuck in."

I followed Harold, with Benji at my side. Two minutes later, Benji was settled by the kitchen door, watching the action with interest, while I wore an oversized apron, the tie wrapped several times around my middle. I wasn't just serving, but dashing around, making toast, scrambling eggs, and doing my best to look like I knew what I was doing.

I was no whizz in the kitchen and always left the cooking to Matthew when home, but I knew how to make the basics. And the bedraggled-looking men, waiting with hungry eyes on the other side of the table, wouldn't mind if the eggs were runny and the toast a little too brown.

"Check the urn!" Harold dashed past me with an armful of plates. "It should be hot enough for the first brews of the day."

I piled loose-leaf tea into several teapots and filled them, steam curling in fragrant tendrils into the air.

The food was laid out, and the men soon accepted plates of fairly presentable breakfast. I was proud of myself. I hadn't burned a single thing.

As the men came to the table and took their food, I looked carefully at them to see if I could spot Charles Blackwood among them, assuming there'd be a family resemblance.

Most were shabbily dressed, with unkempt hair and beards. I didn't see anyone who could be Edmund's brother.

I stopped an older man who was waiting for a refill of tea. "I'm looking for Charles Blackwood. Is he staying here?"

The man's bushy eyebrows lifted and fell several times. "There's a Charles in the end room, the room with the bunk beds. Last time I looked in, he was still sleeping."

I gave the man his tea and an extra slice of toast as a thank you.

Harold walked over and let out a puff of air as he rocked back on his heels. "I appreciate the help. When we put out the plea to the church, we weren't sure who'd step forward. Not everyone is willing to help those who've fallen on hard times."

"I'm always proud to serve," I said.

The door leading into the kitchen opened, and a young man in his twenties bundled through.

"I didn't think you were coming in today!" Harold said.

"I was feeling better and getting under my ma's feet, so she kicked me out. Looks like I've missed the breakfast rush."

"We have Gladys to thank for saving the day," Harold said. "There's plenty of clearing up to do, though."

"It was my absolute pleasure to help." I untied the apron from around my waist. "But I do need to go. Church duties to attend to."

"You're a godsend." Harold heartily shook my hand. "You're welcome back anytime. You and your lady friends."

After nodding at both men, I collected Benji. I glanced over my shoulder to ensure I wasn't being observed, but they were ensconced in the clearing up and didn't notice me head along the corridor towards the sleeping area rather than leaving the building.

I went to the end room and poked my head in. Sure enough, bunk beds lined either side of the walls. One of the lower beds was occupied by a man who was sitting up, blinking and yawning.

"I'm sorry to disturb you, but are you Charles Blackwood?"

He jumped, and his head whipped around to look at me. "How do you know me?"

"I'm from the local church, Gladys," I said sweetly. "Perhaps I could buy you breakfast? I'd like to talk to you about a matter of some urgency."

"What urgency?"

"It's about your brother, Edmund."

Charles yawned loudly. "You said you're from a church?"

"Well, I'm associated with lots of charitable organisations."

He rubbed the back of his neck. "We get a lot of you types around here, trying to save our souls. It's too late for that."

"We never give up on saving the lost lambs," I said. "How about that breakfast?"

Charles smacked his lips together. "Give me a minute. I need to make myself decent."

"I'll wait for you outside." I left Charles to tidy himself and dress.

He ambled out a few minutes later, looking like he'd slept in his clothes. "There's a café along the way I go to when I have a few spare coins. They do an excellent full English."

"Then that's where we'll go."

He kept glancing at me as we walked along, but asked no questions. We settled ourselves in the café. I ordered Charles a full English breakfast, a large pot of tea, and indulged myself in a teacake, even though I wasn't hungry.

"You said you wanted to talk about Edmund?" Charles asked.

"I'm sorry to say, I have bad news about your brother," I said.

"You mean him being dead?"

"Oh... you already know?"

"I heard people talking about a chap who got hit on the head in the Green Man. I lost interest until I heard the name *Edmund*. That's when I learned of it."

"I'm very sorry."

"I appreciate your kindness. We weren't that close, not recently, but he was the only family member who talked to me," Charles said. "As you may have noticed, I'm not swimming in the lap of luxury. I've had a few bad turns, and I'm struggling to get back on my feet, but I will."

"I'm sure you will," I said. "We all find ourselves struggling."

His eyes narrowed. "I can't imagine you've ever struggled much."

"A person's outward appearance shouldn't mean you assume their life is full of delights and joy."

Charles nodded but asked no further questions. "His death shows nothing good comes of making a name for yourself."

"What do you mean by that?" I asked.

"The fancy banking job and all those posh business dinners. Look where it got Edmund. Most likely, a disgruntled customer walloped him because he wouldn't give him a loan."

The door to the café slammed open. A dour-looking type with tattoos on his knuckles strode to our table. Two men lurked outside, obviously his companions.

"Where's my money?" he demanded, jabbing a thick finger against Charles's chest.

Charles reeled back, his face draining of colour. "Mickey! I don't owe you. I paid you everything."

"You didn't pay the interest. And that gets expensive. You pay me what I'm owed, or I'll break something to remind you not to mess with me."

"How very dare you," I said, rising to my feet. "We were in the middle of an important conversation."

Charles shook his head. "Gladys, don't get involved. I'll handle this."

"Who's this? Your old lady?" Mickey sneered at me.

"It doesn't matter who I am," I said, "but it does matter that you're interfering in private business. You need to leave."

"Good luck if she is your old woman," Mickey said in a mocking tone. "Her tongue's too sharp for my taste."

"I'll find you later," Charles muttered to Mickey. "Give you what I owe."

"I'm not falling for that line," Mickey growled. "Now I've got you, you're not getting away, you little sneak. You owe me, and if you don't pay up this second, I'll make you sorry you were ever born."

"I could have you arrested for making threats," I said.

Mickey pivoted towards me, his eyes cold and devoid of emotion. "Since you two seem so friendly, you can pay his debt. What have you got in that bag?" He reached for my handbag, but I reared back and smacked him across the side of the head with it.

He grabbed for me, but I slid out of his way.

"You vicious old maid! You'll regret getting yourself involved," Mickey snarled. "Now you owe me."

"I owe you nothing but a lesson in manners," I snapped.

"Give me your handbag and we'll call it quits," Mickey said. "Depending on how much you've got in there, it might wipe out both your debts."

"You'll get nothing from me."

Mickey launched at me again, and I dodged around the table. All this time, Charles watched with wide-eyed astonishment, not lifting a finger to assist.

Mickey's foul gaze slid to Benji, who'd been quietly lying under the table but now stood alert, growling softly.

"That dog of yours will do. Lads," he called to the men outside, "we've got a new pup to break in."

# Chapter 10

The brute lunged for Benji.

I shoved the café table hard to block him, sending cups crashing and plates spinning. "Don't you dare touch him!"

Benji was on the alert as the men circled him, a growl rumbling in his chest. My boy knew danger when he saw it. Teeth bared, hackles up, he planted himself between me and the thugs.

Mickey swore and came around the table fast. I grabbed the nearest thing, the teapot, still half full, and flung it straight into his face. He screamed, steam rising as scalding tea soaked his clothing.

"You wicked old hag!" he roared, clutching his cheek.

"Call me that again," I said, stepping forward, "and I'll show you wicked. Leave before the police arrive." I flicked a glance at the man behind the counter. Drat. He'd vanished.

One of the other thugs rushed me. I ducked and drove my elbow into his gut then jabbed my knee into his chin as he doubled over. He dropped like a sack of coal, moaning.

Benji tore into the third man with a snarl and a blur of teeth and fur. The man staggered, shouting, trying to shake Benji loose, but my most excellent dog held fast.

"Charles!" I shouted. "A little help?"

He sat frozen, mouth open, eyes wide with shock.

A crash came behind me. It was Mickey again. He swung a chair at me. I sidestepped, but it clipped my shoulder. Pain shot down my arm, and I hissed through my teeth.

I grabbed a fork off the table and held it like a weapon. Mickey advanced again, his face red from my teapot attack. I waited, heart pounding, letting him get close.

He sneered. "You think that little fork's going to stop me?"

I stabbed the fork down into the back of his hand as he reached for me. He jerked back, cradling it against his chest, swearing a string of filth as red blossomed across his knuckles.

Benji lunged past me, launching himself at Mickey's legs. He went down with a thud that rattled the crockery still clinging to the table.

Another thug charged me from behind. I twisted and ducked low. His momentum carried him forward onto the edge of the overturned table. His shins cracked against the wood, and I rammed my shoulder into his chest, knocking him back.

Benji was all fury and teeth now, dancing around Mickey, nipping and snapping, keeping him from rising.

The third man grabbed a metal tray and swung it like a weapon. The tray clipped my arm, the impact spinning me. I lashed out with my foot, catching him in the knee.

He stumbled sideways. I followed it up with a hard kick to his ribs.

He didn't go down. He turned, his face twisted with rage, and tackled me bodily. We crashed into the café counter, sending cutlery and sugar bowls flying. He tried to pin me. I grabbed a butter knife and jabbed it at him, grazing his cheek. He roared, grabbed my wrist, and slammed it down. The knife clattered across the floor.

Behind us, Benji snarled again, a guttural, warning growl. He'd seen I was in trouble. He pelted over and sank his teeth into my attacker's calf.

The man shrieked and kicked wildly. I twisted free, driving my elbow into his jaw.

"Charles!" I shouted again. "Do something!"

Charles had just enough spine to rise to his feet and swing a chair at the thug nearest him. It shattered on impact, but too little, too late. The man turned and floored him with a punch that sent him sprawling.

Mickey rose again. His face was a mask of fury. His speared hand was wrapped in a napkin as he stormed towards me, grabbed a cup off the counter, and swung it at my temple.

Stars exploded behind my eyes, and I went down.

Despite being stunned, I still heard Benji fighting. Brave. Unrelenting. I had to help him, but I kept seeing double as warmth trickled through my hair.

"Get a sack!" someone shouted.

I tried to crawl, tried to reach for Benji, but a boot slammed into my side, once, twice, until I couldn't breathe.

"Get him in. Hold him down. Bloody hell, he bit me—"

"No!" My voice broke. I reached out, fingers brushing the empty floorboards. "Benji!"

As I blinked, my vision snapped into focus just in time to see the sack pulled tight. Benji's furious snarls turned to muffled thrashing.

I caught one last glimpse of the bag writhing violently before the café door was flung open and the men vanished into the grey morning.

Gone.

With my heart.

# Chapter 11

I pulled myself to my feet. My head spun, and I almost fell, but I grabbed the edge of a table and kept myself upright.

"We must follow them. They have Benji," I said. "Somebody help me!"

A chair scraped back, and Charles fumbled off the floor, one hand clamped against his jaw. "The O'Rourke family are ruthless. You can't stop them."

"I will stop them, but I can't do it on my own." I gingerly touched my head, aware of my injury, but still determined to help Benji.

"Missus, maybe this will help." The timid café owner reappeared, holding a gun.

"Why didn't you use that when those men were here?" I demanded.

"I'd never go up against the O'Rourke family," he replied. "They run the gambling dens and illegal fight rings around here. They've got policemen in their pockets. You don't know who you can trust."

"Will you come with me and bring your weapon? I must save Benji," I said.

He shook his head, his hand trembling. "You can have the gun, but that's all the help I'm giving you. If they find out I gave you this gun, they'll burn my café down. Maybe my home, too."

I barely held back my rage at these cowards, my glare flashing from Charles to the café owner. "At least tell me where they're heading."

The men exchanged a nervous glance.

Charles looked out the window. "To the fight ring with your dog."

I drew in a shaky breath as the shocking realisation hit. "By fight ring, you're not talking about men sparring, are you?"

Charles stirred to life. "They're known for it around these parts. Baiting dogs against each other makes them money."

"Grown men betting on which animal will tear the other to pieces?" I hissed out my disgust. "Is that where you've been gambling away your money?"

Charles shook his head. "No! I'm a horse man. But the O'Rourke family have been running rings in this area for years. It was easy for them to collect the strays, especially during the war, when people were tipping out their animals or found themselves homeless and couldn't take their dogs with them."

It sickened me that there were individuals in our society who profited off misery. "You know where they hold the dog fights, don't you?"

Charles gulped but nodded.

"Give me that gun." I gestured at the café owner. "I'm getting Benji back."

He handed over the gun without protest. I hoped I wouldn't have to use it, but if the O'Rourke family refused to return Benji, I'd pull the trigger.

Despite Charles's continued protests as he lagged behind me, I hailed a taxi, ensuring the gun was tucked out of sight in my handbag, and we set off, heading deeper into the slum area of Faversham.

Charles shook beside me, his hands clasped so tightly his fingers were white from where the blood was cut off.

"You don't have to come inside with me," I said. "This is my matter to deal with. I just need to know the location."

"This is madness. You saw what those men can do."

"My head is still pounding from our unfortunate encounter. But they took the one thing from me that I hold most dear. I'll do whatever it takes to rescue Benji."

"It's just a dog. Can't you get another one?" Charles asked.

I whacked him hard on the arm. "He is not just a dog. And the thought of Benji being tossed into a ring and broken so those brutes can use him to make money sickens my stomach, as it should yours if you have an ounce of dignity."

"I don't agree with it," Charles muttered. "But there's nothing we can do. The O'Rourke family runs the dark side of Faversham. They've taken over some old warehouses. They use a bottling factory for the fight, but they have fingers in all the pies."

"They won't for much longer. Not now I'm on to them," I said. "One moment, driver. Stop by that telephone box. You're right, Charles. We need reinforcements, and I know who to contact." I hopped out and placed a call to my office in Margate, but Jacob didn't pick up. He was most likely out on business.

I tried the Green Man and was glad when Colin answered. "It's Veronica. I've little time to explain, so please don't ask questions."

"Right you are, boss," Colin said.

"Benji has been stolen by the O'Rourkes, and I intend to get him back, but I require police assistance."

A strangled sound came down the telephone line. "The O'Rourkes? I see why you need a hand. And you're in luck. Your fella and his police friend stopped by here a few minutes ago. They were looking for you."

I breathed out a sigh of relief. "Tell them to meet me at the disused bottle factory. The O'Rourkes use it to hold dog fights. That's where they've taken Benji. I'm going there now with Edmund's brother to retrieve him."

That same strangled sound came again. "I'll get right on that. You stay safe."

"Thank you, Colin. I intend to, and I intend to get Benji back too."

We swiftly said our goodbyes, and I hopped back in the taxi, ordering the driver to carry on.

Charles was still shaking, but I had little comfort to offer him. He'd got himself into this dreadful mess and done little to help the situation in the café.

"Why would you get yourself involved with such terrible people?" I asked.

Charles was silent for several seconds. "Some say it's an illness. I use my gambling as a distraction. I have... unhappy thoughts. Ever since coming back from the war."

I slid him a glance out of the corner of my eye. "You served?"

"Three years. Some of it on the front line. They're not happy memories. And now, sometimes, I need something to distract me. I'm not proud of it. I wish I could have been more like Edmund. He was one of the lucky ones. He had a bad chest, which meant he couldn't join up. He never understood what it was like. I tried to explain it to him, but he told me to pull myself together. So, I found a way to manage."

My fury at Charles faded somewhat. "It was a most unpleasant time. I've seen firsthand the lingering aftereffects caused by the terrors men went through."

"You had family who served?"

"I served myself," I said.

Charles's curious gaze swept over me. "With your character, I see how you'd be an asset."

"This is as far as I go," the cabbie said. "I know who runs these buildings, so I don't want to be seen helping you. The bottle factory is at the end of this row."

I paid the cabbie, not angry with him for being too afraid to involve himself in these dealings, and stepped out of the vehicle with Charles.

"Shouldn't we wait for your police friends to get here?" Charles whispered as we hurried towards the glass factory, a broken-down building with smashed windows and a sagging roof.

"They're not far away," I replied.

A loud crash echoed inside the factory, followed by a vicious bark. Benji!

I took off running, drawing the gun from my handbag and gripping it firmly. A glance over my shoulder showed

Charles had barely moved, frozen with indecision. If he was no use to me, I'd leave him behind.

Rather than storm through the open main door, I slipped around the side of the factory and located a smaller door at the back. I eased it open and peered inside. The sight before me turned my stomach.

There were a dozen cages, some holding dogs in appalling conditions with untreated wounds, barely any food or water, and filthy floors.

I made a silent vow to every one of them that I'd do whatever it took to ensure their safety and free them from this horror.

Several dogs barked as I crept past, but when they realised I wasn't there to hurt them, they settled. One or two even wagged their tails. Dogs were extraordinary creatures, so full of kindness and forgiveness. Even after all they'd endured at the hands of the O'Rourke family, they were willing to trust a human. I'd make sure that trust, that unwavering loyalty, was rewarded.

A familiar bark rang out. Benji was fighting back.

I hurried through the room to another door, slightly ajar. I peered through the gap.

The men who'd taken Benji were inside. He was chained, snarling and lunging at them with wild fury. Each time they approached, he bared his teeth. One of the men held a wicked-looking cudgel, edging closer.

I had no time to wait for Jacob and Bishop. If I didn't act, it would be too late. I stepped into the room, gun raised. The sharp click of the hammer being cocked echoed around the space.

All three men turned.

"I should warn you, I'm an excellent shot. Take another step towards my dog, and it'll be your last."

"You had the cheek to follow us. You can't have a brain in that head of yours," Mickey O'Rourke sneered.

I tensed, finger tightening on the trigger. "Unchain my dog."

A soft sound came from behind me, and I whirled around. It was Charles. His courage had found him at last. He held a hefty piece of wood like a makeshift club, pale but determined.

Even with Charles at my side, we were outnumbered, and my darling Benji was out of reach.

"You can't shoot us all," Mickey said with a sneer.

"I'll do my best. Now, who wants to go first? Which one of you is ready to die over a dog?"

"You can't be here just because of that dog," Mickey said.

"Unchain Benji," I said, "and perhaps we can have a civil conversation. Get your man to drop that cudgel, or he'll be the first to feel the sting of a bullet."

Mickey scowled at me, then gestured for his lackey to drop the weapon. The cudgel clattered to the floor.

"That's a good start," I said.

"What do we have to be civil about?" Mickey growled at me.

My gaze flicked between Benji and Mickey. "Charles's brother recently died, and we're investigating what happened to him."

"Investigating?" Mickey snorted. "You're not a copper. I'd know your face if you were local."

"It's a private investigation," I replied, keeping the gun steady. "But I work closely with the local police."

"Speaking to old Charlie boy there won't help you," Mickey said with a grunt. "He only cares about one thing. How he'll scrape up a few pennies to place on his next horse. The man's obsessed. It's good for my business, but not for him."

"You still haven't unchained Benji." My voice hardened. "It makes me think you'd rather I shoot you. Shall I aim for an arm or a leg? Whichever is injured, sepsis will soon set in thanks to how filthy this place is."

Mickey sucked in air through his teeth, clearly irritated. "It's a shame you're not a man. With that smart mouth and lack of fear, you'd make a good fighter in the ring."

I glared at him and adjusted my stance. The gun was growing heavy, but I refused to lower it. "If you value your life, let my dog go unharmed."

"We shouldn't have bothered. He'd never be a prime fighter," Mickey muttered. "Too small."

"Benji is an excellent dog." My voice trembled only slightly. "He fights for what matters."

Benji growled fiercely as one of the men unclipped the chain from around his neck. Then my beloved dog was flying across the floor, his paws barely touching the cold concrete, before launching into my arms and almost knocking me over.

I held him close, joy surging through me. He licked my cheek, whisking away the single tear that had slipped free and revealed my gut-churning fear.

One of Mickey's men shifted, perhaps emboldened by my distraction. I raised the gun instantly.

"Don't attempt any foolish bravery. I can shoot one-handed." I set Benji down, and he pressed close to my leg, his body taut, ready to fight if needed. "Now you have seen sense, let's have that conversation. How much does Charles owe you?"

"You can see from the state of him that the man has nothing," Mickey said. "He's been avoiding me. I collect my debts weekly, and he's three weeks overdue."

"He said he paid what he owed."

"That's the trouble with these types," Mickey spat. "They never read the terms. I told him to pay back what I loaned him and the interest."

"Which I suppose is extortionate," I said.

"It's not my fault Charlie boy got himself in a mess," Mickey replied. "He's a desperate man. A sad man."

I glanced at Charles. His head was lowered, his cheeks flushed with shame. If he was that desperate for money, could he have gone after Edmund? Would he have been desperate enough to kill his brother if refused help?

"I thought we had you the other night," Mickey said, snapping my attention back to him. "But you're fast on your feet."

"The other night?" I asked. "What happened?"

"We almost caught Charlie boy," Mickey said. "But he made a run for it. We stalked him through the streets of Faversham for hours before giving up around midnight. Decided he wasn't worth the trouble. Isn't that right, lads?"

The men around him grunted in agreement.

"That was the night Edmund died," Charles said quietly. "It's why I went into hiding. I wanted to talk to the police about what happened, but it was too risky. The O'Rourke family has insiders in the police, and I didn't want anyone tipping them off that I was nearby. They'd give me a thrashing."

"The O'Rourke family is your alibi?" I said, stunned.

Charles nodded slowly. "I didn't want Edmund dead. I've asked him for help in the past, and he gave me cash, but he refused the last time and said giving me money would only make things worse. After he knocked me back a few times, I gave up. I was on my own. That's why we drifted apart."

"You were disappointed by his refusal to help fuel your gambling addiction," I said. "Your brother was helping you, trying to free you from these monsters."

"It didn't feel like it," Charles murmured. "But I wasn't anywhere near the Green Man when Edmund was killed. I was running from Mickey and his brothers. It wasn't me."

The front door of the bottle factory slammed open. Jacob, Bishop, and several policemen charged in. The O'Rourkes tensed, ready to fight, but they were quickly overwhelmed despite a fierce struggle and a miasma of foul cursing.

Jacob rushed over and pulled me into an embrace. I was happy to hand the gun off to him, my arm trembling from the strain of holding it steady for so long.

"You should have waited for us," he said.

"Benji was in trouble. There was no time," I replied.

Jacob crouched beside Benji and patted him gently. "He's not injured."

"He was so brave." I stroked Benji's head. "He fought them every inch of the way. We'll have to buy him a steak dinner as a reward."

"Benji may not be injured, but you are." Jacob's gaze flicked to the side of my head, worry etched across his face. "You need to see a doctor."

"I will," I promised. "But first, we have a dozen desperate dogs who need our help."

# Chapter 12

I stared into the fire at the Green Man, letting the heat seep into my bones. The doctor had cleaned the cut on my head and declared it shallow but messy. I'd needed three stitches and a stern lecture about not ignoring the warning signs of a concussion. I'd nodded politely and made all the right promises.

"Are you sure you're comfortable?" Jacob hovered by the chair. "You should be lying down. Maybe you need something to eat. Or tea. Have you had any tea?"

"For heaven's sake, Jacob," I snapped, turning to glare at him. "If you flap any harder, you'll lift off the ground."

He gave me a wounded look and set the tea tray he carried down on the table beside me with exaggerated care.

I winced, instantly regretful. "I'm sorry. That wasn't fair. I'm just tired. And I want an update on how the dogs are faring. It's been hours since we delivered them to the vet. We should know how they're doing by now."

Jacob sat in the chair opposite mine and gave me one of his steady looks, the kind that made me feel like a wayward child who'd been caught filching biscuits.

"I know you're tired," he said gently. "And sore. And stubborn. But I'd rather fuss over you than find you bleeding in some horrible ruin of a building."

"Point taken." I reached for the tea, cradling the warm cup in my hands.

"And I had word from the vet while you were dozing. I thought you needed rest, so I didn't disturb you."

"Oh! How are they? Will they all pull through?"

Jacob's face lit up. "All of them. The vet called in extra staff to treat them."

I let out a breath. "Good. That's good. And tell him no expense spared. After everything they've been through, they deserve the best."

"Apparently, a few were even wagging their tails when they got their food."

Despite demanding to take the dogs to the vet myself, Jacob had put his foot down and insisted I receive medical attention while he and Colin looked after them. Colin knew a local vet with an excellent reputation, and he'd used the pub's van to load in the dogs and take them there.

A smile tugged at the corners of my mouth. "We'll find homes for them. I'll make sure of it. They can be our first intake at the new centre. Although we have yet to finalise that centre. I should telephone Lord Faversham. Maybe this situation will speed up matters and he'll commit to donating his land."

Jacob pressed a restraining hand on my arm. "Not yet. You must rest. And the dogs won't be leaving the vets for days. They need time to recover, just like you. Lord Faversham will be there in the morning."

I wanted to protest, but I was bone weary, my head hurt, and Benji was comfortable, stretched out across my feet, gently snoring, making it impossible for me to move.

A familiar figure wrapped in a long coat and damp from the evening mist stepped inside the pub.

"Bishop!" Jacob said, raising a hand to acknowledge him. "I didn't expect to see you until the morning."

Bishop walked over and shrugged off his coat. "I thought you'd appreciate an update since we're holding half the O'Rourke gang in the cells." His eyes flicked to me. "Veronica. You like to keep life interesting, don't you? How's the head feeling?"

"Healing nicely. What news?"

"This can wait until the morning," Jacob protested. "Veronica needs to rest."

"Bishop is here! It won't take a moment. And I won't be able to rest until I have a full update."

Jacob sighed. "I'll fetch some drinks. Make sure she stays in her chair."

"She is quite capable of seeing to her own needs," I bit back.

Bishop chuckled as he settled into a seat. "Jacob is only worried about you. He wants to keep you safe."

I held in a tart retort. "I know. When one has been independent for a long time, it's hard to accept help. Although I'm glad your help arrived in the nick of time."

"You'll be questioned about that gun," Bishop said. "Will you reveal where you got it from?"

"That knowledge has slipped out of my memory. It must be because of the bump on the head. But rest assured, I only point guns at people who richly deserve it," I said.

Bishop gave a low whistle and shook his head. "You got lucky. Mickey O'Rourke is not just any thug. He's influential, slippery, and mean as a cornered rat. Most people steer clear unless they want their kneecaps introduced to a cricket bat."

"It wasn't luck. I know how to protect myself. And no one takes Benji and gets away with it. He's family."

Benji, sensing the attention, gave a soft huff in his sleep. All the excitement had tired him out.

"Still, it was a risk. The kind of thing that ends with headlines or headstones. You're not trained for—"

"Oh, for heaven's sake," I cut in. "I don't need training to know how to point a gun. I needed my dog back. End of story. And why do you think I have no firearms training?"

Jacob returned with a tray of drinks for us. Nothing alcoholic for me, just another strong cup of tea and some biscuits. "Veronica served during the war. She got up to all sorts, but rarely talks about it."

"It doesn't do to gossip or brag about that time," I said. "We did what was necessary and achieved the desired outcome. That is all that matters."

"So," Bishop said, after a sip of his drink, "you said Charles Blackwood was hiding not because he was guilty of murdering Edmund, but because he was scared for his life, thanks to Mickey and his crooked cronies."

"Charles is innocent. They were chasing him through the streets the evening his brother was murdered."

"We've known about their antics for years. There are more than a few unsolved murders where Mickey is a suspect. Lately, he's been more into intimidation and getting people into debt, so they owe him."

"Do you have enough to keep them off the streets?" I asked.

Bishop leaned forward, resting his forearms on his knees. "We're holding them. They were caught red-handed at the bottle factory, so there's no wriggling out of that. The dog fighting ring alone is enough to see them face charges."

Jacob gave a satisfied grunt. "From all accounts, it's long overdue they end up behind bars."

"We found more than the dogs," Bishop continued. "While searching the back rooms, we turned up a cache of stolen goods. Jewellery, silverware, even a crate of expensive spirits we believe was pinched off a delivery bound for London. And some of it matches recent reports from housebreaks across the county."

I sat up a little straighter. "I heard they have their fingers in plenty of unsavoury pies."

"With any luck, they'll spend a long stretch behind bars, and Kent will be better for it," Bishop said. "Veronica, I'll need a statement from you. You can press charges for the assault. Edmund's brother, too."

"How is Charles?" I asked. "I wasn't sure I could trust the chap, but he came good at the last minute."

"He's also spending a night in the cells. I took pity on him when he said he had nowhere else to go. He's got a belly full of food and warm blankets. He's safe there until we can fix him up somewhere stable in the morning."

"That's decent of you," I said. "The man has fallen on hard times."

"I also need to interview him about Edmund's death."

"I assure you, he's innocent," I said.

"Let me be the judge of that."

I opened my mouth to protest, but a wave of exhaustion hit. Bishop was a sensible chap, so he wouldn't get things in a muddle.

Bishop scratched the back of his neck. "I'll be busy tomorrow, speaking to all these suspects and getting their statements."

Jacob gave a low huff. "Does that mean we're back to square one on figuring out what happened to Edmund?"

"Not quite," I said. "We've ruled someone out. That's progress."

Bishop gave me a look that was equal parts exasperated and amused. "You're too cheerful for someone who nearly got their head bashed in by a bunch of thugs."

I shrugged. "I'm not cheerful. I'm determined. There's still a murderer out there, and I fully intend to find them. This murder occurred in my pub, and that's unacceptable. Besides, there are more suspects to consider."

Bishop raised a brow. "Go on, then. Who do you fancy for this murder?"

"Florence Hatley."

Bishop made a noise of disbelief before I'd even finished the name. "She's an old spinster with poor eyesight. Don't be ridiculous."

I fixed him with a look. "She sees perfectly well, as her curtain twitching revealed to me. And spite is a powerful motivator."

"She's seventy if she's a day," Bishop added.

"Miss Hatley holds a grudge against the Blackwoods," I said. "Edmund's ancestors swindled her family out of a fortune. She's never forgiven them. And she still lives in the crumbling cottage opposite this pub. It's not suitable for such an elderly woman. Unless she's not as fragile as you believe her to be. The pub is a hop, skip, and a jump from her front door."

Bishop chuckled. "Even if Miss Hatley hated Edmund, she couldn't have bludgeoned him. It's more likely she'd curse him with bad luck or bore him to death with the family history."

"That's uncalled for." I didn't laugh. "You'd be surprised what someone can accomplish when fuelled by vengeance and a lifetime of bitterness. She's a spry old thing. Be sure you check with the lady who takes in her meals to ensure she was there at the time of the murder."

They looked unconvinced, so I changed tack. "What about May Shaw? We saw how dismissive she was of Edmund's interests. And when I researched the Blackwood family history, I found some of May's ancestors were merchants who lost their land and livelihood just before the Blackwoods became conveniently wealthy."

Bishop nodded slowly. "Edmund's ancestors stole from May's family, too?"

"They made it a habit. Perhaps it wasn't direct theft, but through land grabs, suspicious debts, forged ledgers. It's documented in the archives that the families weren't fond of each other. May is sharp enough to have traced any unfairness against her family and perhaps angry enough to have done something about it."

Jacob frowned into his ale. "What are you thinking? This is some long game? A revenge plot finally coming to fruition?"

"May failed to mention the old family feud when we spoke and the fact she'd been seen in many heated arguments with Edmund," I said.

Bishop leaned back, his expression thoughtful. "That's a leap from ancient grudges to murder."

"Maybe," I said. "But if we keep discounting people because they don't fit the usual mould, we'll miss something important. Or someone."

Jacob reached for the fire poker, jabbing the logs. "I miss the days when crimes were committed by obvious villains in black cloaks."

"Criminals can wear cardigans and carry library cards," I said. "Cads and rotters come in all shapes and sizes. Some even look like little old ladies or sensible archivists."

The conversation drifted on, the warm glow of the fire softening the sharp edges of theory and accusation until my thoughts grew sluggish and my bones heavier than lead.

Benji shifted on my feet, letting out a snuffling snore. I glanced down and ran my fingers through the ruff of fur behind his ears. He barely stirred, content as a cat in sunshine.

I leaned back with a sigh. What a day! Mystery, mayhem, and dogs. At least the dogs were safe. I'd be on to that in the morning. Those innocent angels deserved the perfect forever homes after everything they'd been through.

Jacob turned, and I caught the movement through slitted lids as I fought against tiredness. "That yawn was so large your jaw cracked. Come on. Time for bed."

"I decide on my bedtime. I'm not a child," I murmured, though the words lacked any sting.

"You've had a head injury and been through enough excitement for a whole year. You're going to your lodgings. I'll sleep on the sofa to make sure that head injury isn't serious."

"The scandal," I said in a mock gasp. "What will the townsfolk think of an unmarried man escorting me home?"

He didn't smile. "Let them talk. You're my girl, and I'm protecting you, even if you don't want me to."

"I'm a grown woman who can attend to her own needs." Although something about the way Jacob said those words, gruff and steady and very sure, settled in my chest like a warm stone. So, I didn't argue anymore.

I sat up carefully, mindful of the tender throb behind my temple. Jacob was already on his feet, scooping up our coats with his usual efficient energy. Benji blinked awake as I shifted, gave a huff of disapproval at being dragged away from the delicious fire, and then promptly followed me, tail wagging.

Bishop walked us to the door, the cool night air wrapping around us as we stepped outside. "I'll head back to the station, see how things are shaping up," he said. "But if anything stirs in that sharp mind of yours overnight, you'll let me know?"

"Of course," I said, clasping his hand briefly. "Goodnight, Bishop. And thank you for everything you've done today."

"Night, Veronica. Jacob." He walked off into the darkness.

Jacob fell into step beside me, one hand hovering at my back, ready to catch me if I stumbled. I wouldn't, but I liked knowing he was there.

As we reached the quiet lane that led to my bed-and-breakfast, I glanced up at the stars and took a slow breath. My body ached, my thoughts were a tangle, and there were more questions than answers. But at least we were moving in the right direction.

"After a good night's rest," I said, more to myself than to Jacob, "we'll set the world to rights. And the dogs will be my first priority."

# Chapter 13

I woke with every inch of my body feeling as if an especially aggressive Shire horse had trampled me. My head throbbed with a dull, persistent ache that pulsed in time with my heartbeat, and my limbs protested every movement.

I sat up, groaning softly and taking a moment to make sure everything worked. Bruises always felt worse the day after the injury happened.

A moment later, Jenny bustled in without so much as a knock, her apron already dusted with flour and her cheeks pink with righteous activity.

"Oh, you're up!" she declared, sounding scandalised and delighted. "I was just coming to check on you. I told Jacob you'd need at least another hour, poor lamb. 'Stubborn as a mule,' he said, and I said, 'Well, aren't they all?'"

I blinked blearily. "Good morning, Jenny."

"Is it?" she replied, hands on hips. "I'm not sure it is, not with you looking like you've been dragged backwards through a hedge. And what's this about Jacob staying the night? Not that I mind. He's a nice enough lad, and I trust him. He told me he was a policeman. Is that true?"

"It is. Well, he used to be. And thank you for letting him sleep on your sofa."

"I had little choice! I was scared half to death when I came into the sitting room in my robe and slippers, and there he was! I almost hit him with a candlestick."

"Sorry for the shock. You were already in bed when we came in last night. He refused to leave, given I had a little incident."

"From the mess of that face, it was more than a little incident. Don't you worry. I can get past the neighbours going all a-twitter when it gets out that a man stayed here, so long as you tell me everything."

"Let them twitter," I muttered, pushing back the covers. "It was all perfectly innocent."

"I should hope so." She sniffed. "You're a respectable woman, after all. He was very attentive, I must say. Slept on the sofa but poked his head in here every few hours to check you were breathing. Sweet, really."

I swung my legs out of bed and winced. "That sounds about right."

"So, tell me everything." Jenny stood in front of me, set firm.

I swiftly realised I'd get no breakfast until I'd recounted yesterday's adventures, so I did just that, accompanied by gasps and startled squeaks from Jenny.

"What a terrible thing," she declared once I'd finished. "Come down and eat. I've made sausages, bacon, eggs, the works. And there's a pot of tea with your name on it. That'll get the spring back in your step."

By the time I'd washed, dressed, and made it to the kitchen table, Jacob was already there, hair damp from a wash, his shirt sleeves rolled to the elbows. He stood when he saw me and pulled out a chair.

"You look terrible," he said cheerfully.

"I've always adored your charm." I eased myself down with a wince.

Jenny clattered a plate down in front of me. "Eat that. Gracious! In the cold light of day, you look like you've been in a war."

"She has been through it," Jacob muttered, observing me as if I were a zoo specimen.

"I'm sitting right here. Ask me how I feel rather than making assumptions due to my outer appearance. And since you're both curious, I'm fine," I said, not that either of them would believe me. "After breakfast, I want to check on the dogs."

Jacob arched an eyebrow. "You're still recovering."

"They're our responsibility," I insisted. "And besides, I won't rest until I've seen them for myself."

Jenny patted my shoulder. "Eat first. Argue after. I'll fetch the jam for the toast. You can't plan anything on an empty stomach."

Jacob watched me butter a thick slice of toast as if I might collapse face-first onto the plate at any moment. "You're not going out today."

I bit into the toast with what I hoped was an air of confidence and not someone whose head pulsed like a faulty steam engine. "I feel perfectly fine."

"Untrue," he muttered, reaching for his tea.

"I beg your pardon?"

"You winced getting into the chair. You winced buttering your toast. You winced when Jenny patted your shoulder. You're a walking bruise! You're sore, you've got stitches in your head, and if I had my way, you'd be tucked up on the sofa with Benji and a hot water bottle."

As if summoned, Benji let out a deep, theatrical whine from the rug near the cooker, his soulful eyes flicking towards Jacob before returning to me.

"Benji agrees with me. He knows we have to see the dogs," I said.

Benji thumped his tail against the floor in endorsement.

Jacob leaned forward on his elbows. "Veronica. You were attacked yesterday and stitched up by the local doctor. You deserve one day off."

I dropped my voice and reached for his hand. "The dogs need us. They were chained, beaten, and terrified. I want them to see something different now. I want them to see kindness."

Jacob sighed, long and low. "You make it hard to argue when you become so noble."

"Good," I said, taking another bite of toast. "Because I'm going. With or without you. I would prefer your company, but if you don't want to be noble with me and Benji..."

Benji let out an encouraging woof and lifted one paw.

"Traitor," Jacob muttered at him.

I smiled. "Then it's agreed. After breakfast, we visit the dogs. Now eat that sausage before Benji steals it from your plate."

The remains of our breakfast were eaten in a companionable silence, and I finally relaxed after yesterday's ordeal. I hadn't liked to admit it, but I'd been terrified. Not for my safety, but for Benji. I sometimes got so embroiled in life's complexities, I forgot what really mattered. The simple things. Family. Friends. Compassion.

Jacob pushed back his chair and stood abruptly.

"Are you going somewhere?" I asked.

His smile had a conspiratorial edge to it. "You stay here. I'll be back soon."

"From where?"

"With so many dogs in need of care, I knew you wouldn't rest, even though you need to."

My gaze narrowed. "What are you up to?"

His smile widened. "You'll soon find out. Finish your tea."

I was tempted to hasten after him to see what shenanigans were afoot, but my aching limbs kept me in my seat and sipping my tea, with Benji by my side.

I finished another round of toast, supplied by Jenny, and had drunk two cups of tea and fed Benji a bacon rind when Jacob finally returned. And he wasn't alone.

I gasped in delight and surprise. "Molly! Whatever brings you here?"

"As if you don't know." Molly Banbury bustled over, her wild curls barely contained by her eye-patch band. She engulfed me in an enormous hug then pulled back and cast a critical gaze over me. "Whatever have you got yourself into? That's the beginning of a black eye. And your head is stitched!"

"Only three tiny stitches," I said. "It's nothing to worry about."

"I was worried when I got the telephone call from Jacob when I was at the shelter. Although not so much about you, since you can hold your own in any situation," Molly said. "But when I heard about the dogs, I came straight here. And I've brought three volunteers."

"Oh, you wonderful creature!" I impulsively hugged Molly again. Molly was a long-time supporter and employee of the dogs' home in Battersea. She could always be relied upon and never flapped.

"I was outraged when I heard about those poor dogs. People who use dogs in such a way..." Molly shook her head. "They ought to be put out of their misery. Jacob told me all about it. He also told me what happened to you. At least some of it. I had to come."

"I'm glad you did. The dogs were taken to the vet and have been there overnight." I glanced at Jacob.

"I telephoned the vet a short while ago," he said. "The dogs are all healing. Some of the injuries are serious, but there are no infections. They need time, nourishment, and a safe space to recover."

"Which is where we come in," Molly said. "It's all arranged. I know people down this way, and they're happy to put me and the other volunteers up for as long as we need until we figure things out."

My heart warmed as Molly told me about her adventure on the train with some of the wonderful volunteers from the dogs' home in Battersea.

"We need a plan of action," I said. "The vet won't want to keep the dogs for long. We must find them somewhere quiet and secure where they can recover."

"You have us for as long as you need us," Molly said. "And we're excited to see our new location. Is it almost ready?"

"Almost." I nodded as an idea formed. "But I need to make a telephone call."

Jenny bustled in, and Molly and Jenny exchanged polite introductions. Tea was poured as I excused myself to make an important call.

Lord Faversham's butler answered the telephone, and I waited a moment until Lord Faversham came on the line.

"Veronica! I'm glad you made contact. I've been thinking about your situation."

"I hope you consider it *our* situation. I'm sure you know I'm eager to move forward with plans to expand the dogs' home. We ran into a diversion at the Green Man, but I trust that won't slow the plans."

He cleared his throat. "About that. It seems you have an awful lot to manage."

I didn't like the nervous note in his voice. "Life is challenging, but we rise and face it, especially when tackling injustice."

"Indeed. But I wonder if you're taking on too much with these plans for an extra shelter."

"I don't consider it a burden, and I don't bear it alone," I said. "As you know, we have a wonderful board of trustees who manages our work in Battersea, and a team of able volunteers, including vets who give their time for free to ensure the animals are well cared for."

"Yes, but that is in London, which is some distance away."

"We have the logistics figured out," I said firmly. "We've been recruiting local volunteers and have a ready team eager to go. We just need the land and the buildings, which is where you come in. You won't have to lift a finger to assist."

"I'm still unsure," Lord Faversham said.

"What will you do with those stables and the land, if not donate them to help abandoned animals? I know how much you adore dogs."

"Of course! I was raised with dogs. My mother once said I preferred the company of dogs and running about like a wild animal in the woods to any worthwhile education."

"Outdoor pursuits are one of the finest ways to educate a child," I said.

He chuckled. "I agree with you there. It did me no harm. Let me think about it some more. I don't want you to be overburdened."

I suppressed a huff of frustration. Was Lord Faversham saying this because I was a woman? He must know how capable I am. We'd had numerous conversations, exchanged dozens of letters, and he'd met the dogs' home trustees and had a tour of our London shelter. He knew what we could achieve.

"Do you not consider me capable?" I asked.

"My dear lady, you can achieve anything you set your mind to."

"Then what is the issue?" I paused. "Is this because of the murder at the Green Man?"

Silence ensued.

I pressed on. "You have nothing to concern yourself with. Everything is in hand with that matter. The police have a list of suspects and are pursuing the evidence."

"As are you," Lord Faversham said on a sigh. "Veronica, I am a man of considerable means, and anyone I intend to go into business with, I thoroughly investigate."

I gritted my teeth. "And what have your investigations uncovered about me?"

"You're a woman with a wild spirit. And that spirit gets you into trouble."

"Not serious trouble," I said cautiously.

"I've been informed about your altercation with the O'Rourke family. They're a troublesome bunch, and I don't want to become entangled with any aspect of what they do."

"I assure you, the O'Rourkes aren't a problem. They're behind bars, and there are no plans to set them free. The police have a lengthy list of charges to bring against them."

"Such criminal enterprises have connections everywhere. Just because you've removed the main aggravators doesn't mean the trouble will stop."

"They'd be foolish to go up against such a man of influence."

Lord Faversham huffed a laugh. "Chaps like that have no boundaries. I'm unsure it's wise for us to work together. I know it's a disappointment, but I'll ask in my social circles and see if anyone has suitable property you may use."

My hand clenched into a fist. "This is nonsense! We desperately need that land."

"With everything going on in your life and work, and the trouble at the pub, this is for the best."

"You're wrong. And I'll prove it to you. I'll see you at the stables in an hour. Goodbye, Lord Faversham." I set down the telephone before he protested.

I'd make this stubborn-headed man see sense. We would take our case to his door and show him what he'd be abandoning.

I returned to the kitchen to find Molly drinking tea while giving Benji's belly a rub.

"It's action stations." I clapped my hands together. "Jacob, please telephone the vet. Find out if any of the dogs are suitable to move and if they have a friendly nature."

His brow furrowed. "The vet said several dogs can leave today, although not the ones with bite wounds. Why do you need them?"

"Lord Faversham's spine is weak. We need to strengthen it with direct action."

"He's the posh type who's giving us the stables and land?" Molly asked.

"He is. But he needs to see how important this work is. He's wobbling."

Molly thumped down her cup. "We'll show him a thing or two."

"Are you sure this is a good idea?" Jacob murmured. "Lord Faversham is a man of influence."

"It's the best idea. We need a home for those dogs, and we need it now. We can't have Lord Faversham changing his mind at such a crucial juncture. Make that telephone call while I get ready. There's no time to waste," I said.

An hour later, we pulled up in the disused stable yard on Lord Faversham's vast estate. Settled on the backseat of the car were Molly, three small, rather bedraggled-looking dogs we'd rescued from the O'Rourkes' clutches, and Benji.

I'd been delighted to see how well the dogs had fared overnight. Although timid, after spending a little time getting to know them and offering plenty of treats, they'd wagged their tails and trusted us enough to jump into the car.

Benji had helped. He was always a stalwart supporter. Whenever there was a nervous dog who needed assistance in finding their paws, he politely nudged, sniffed, and demonstrated we were safe to be around.

Molly ensured the dogs had secure leads before opening the back door and climbing out with them. "These poor little things weren't fighters. They were bait," she muttered, lips pursed with distaste.

"Play that up to Lord Faversham," I said. "We must convince him to give us this land."

"Here he comes." Jacob slid out of the driver's seat and let Benji out.

Lord Faversham drove a sturdy Leyland truck that looked like it had seen service during the war. He climbed out wearing Wellington boots, a warm-weather parka, and a flat cap. He was the epitome of a country gentleman. He strode over, looking grim and determined.

"Miss Vale, I don't appreciate being hung up on when we were mid-conversation," he said.

"Let me introduce you to Molly." I kept my tone polite. "She came down from London with several volunteers. She's worked at the dogs' home and has kept us organised with her excellent skills for years."

Manners overtook him, and Lord Faversham shook Molly's hand. "It's a pleasure to meet you. You do excellent work."

"And we'll do even better work now we have your generous donation of land," Molly said.

"As I was telling Veronica before she so abruptly ended our conversation, now isn't the right time to set up a shelter." Lord Faversham's gaze ran over me several times, and he took a step back. "Are you quite well?"

I'd arranged my hair to hide the stitches, but there was little I could do about the facial bruising. If only Ruby were here to work her makeup magic.

"Nothing a few good nights' sleep won't cure," I said briskly. "And I'm focused on the dogs who desperately need help. Just yesterday, we rescued a dozen caged and injured animals. They were being used in illegal dog fights."

Lord Faversham startled. "That can't be happening around here. This town is respectable."

"I found the dogs. With the assistance of the police, we rescued them, and they've been receiving overnight care."

Lord Faversham's gaze dropped to the three dogs sitting quietly by Molly's feet. "Those dogs are not fighting animals. They use brutes. The ones with muscles."

"They use the smaller dogs as bait," Molly said with a disgusted huff. "These poor little creatures would have been tossed into a ring, and the fighting dogs encouraged to destroy them. It riles them up and gives them bloodlust, so when the fight begins, it's brutal."

"We had to rescue them. Now they need a safe place. A place where they'll never feel fear or pain again," I said, wanting to hug Molly for giving such a glorious speech.

Lord Faversham shook his head, his expression determined. "It makes my blood boil to hear of such things. We're supposed to be a nation of animal lovers. This is a disgrace."

"Let's prove we're a nation of animal lovers," I said. "Donate this land and your stables. These dogs will be the first residents. We already have money from our fundraising activities, so we can get the accommodation ready in a matter of hours. Give these dogs the haven they desperately deserve. Their happy ending rests in your hands."

"Veronica is extremely capable of achieving such a task in a speedy manner," Jacob said. "I learned that the hard way when I doubted her."

Lord Faversham stared at the three little dogs, then he turned and looked over his shoulder, where his chunky, healthy, and happy Labradors played together.

I waited, holding my breath, as he warred with his thoughts.

One of the small dogs gave a soft bark and limped towards Lord Faversham, wagging his scruffy tail. He stopped in front of him and peered up. Lord Faversham crouched and spent a moment letting the dog sniff his hand. The dog licked his hand and nuzzled against his palm.

Lord Faversham looked up at me. "Very well. I am powerless to resist. You may have this land and the stables as per our original agreement."

Molly beamed brightly, and I exhaled in relief.

"You've just changed so many dogs' lives for the better," I said. "You won't regret your decision."

"I hope not. Now, how about a drink to celebrate?" Lord Faversham asked.

Although I'd have preferred to go back to my lodgings and tuck myself into bed for the rest of the morning, it would have been impolite to refuse, especially since this entire deal had almost crumbled.

"I'll take the dogs and inspect the stables," Molly said, already marching off. Nothing made her happier than being busy and following her passion.

We left our vehicle and climbed into Lord Faversham's Leyland. He whisked us back to his grand manor house, which sat on a slight hill providing glorious views across his estate.

The dogs tumbled out in a bundle of excited barking, and Benji raced off with the Labradors, thoroughly enjoying himself.

"Don't worry about them getting in trouble," Lord Faversham said as he watched the dogs go. "The land is fenced and secure, and I have gardeners working most days. They keep an eye on things. The dogs will come inside when they get hungry."

The manor house was as grand as you'd expect from a man of Lord Faversham's breeding. Elegant without being fussy. The hallway was wide, with a high ceiling and a chandelier that looked like it had seen at least three coronations. Oil paintings of countryside scenes lined the walls, and a long Persian runner muffled our footsteps.

He guided us through to a smart parlour, small by manor house standards, panelled in oak and lined with shelves filled with books, old cricket trophies, and framed black-and-white photographs of various notable members of Faversham's elite society.

"Please, sit." Lord Faversham gestured to a pair of leather armchairs near the open fireplace. "I'll have Alfred bring us something."

No sooner had we settled than the butler appeared, a tall, thin man with a face that suggested he'd seen everything and judged none of it worthy of reaction. He poured three generous glasses of something golden and smooth and vanished again.

Lord Faversham raised his glass. "To new beginnings."

I sipped politely, letting the warmth calm the dull throb in my temple. My gaze wandered around the room, but I was drawn to a glass-fronted cabinet near the window. Inside, nestled on green velvet, was a small but dazzling collection of gold coins.

"May I?" I asked, already rising to inspect.

"Of course," Lord Faversham said, clearly pleased. "You have a fine eye, Miss Vale. That's my latest indulgence. Roman aurei, mostly. Beautiful pieces."

I admired the intricate designs, the worn profiles of long-dead emperors, the faded Latin inscriptions, the sheer gleam of them. I wasn't one for razzle dazzle, but these artefacts were a delight.

"They're incredible," I said. "Where did you get them?"

"From Edmund Blackwood."

# Chapter 14

"I thought Edmund was only interested in finding smuggled treasures," I said. "Were these Roman coins found in the tunnel?"

"No. When Edmund got started, he was into all sorts. He told me he found those coins in a field using a metal detector. He kept them because he assumed they'd be worth money, but he wasn't sure how much." Lord Faversham set down his glass and joined me by the cabinet. "I've bought a few other items from him if you'd like to see them."

"Absolutely," I said.

Lord Faversham left the room to retrieve more of his collection.

I raised an eyebrow at Jacob. "I didn't realise Edmund and Lord Faversham were in business together."

"Quiet those racing thoughts," Jacob cautioned.

"We must pursue all avenues when injustice is underway. Even if that avenue is lined with gold, manor houses, and blue blood."

"You're the man's alibi!"

I wrinkled my nose. True enough. Lord Faversham had been in the Green Man before I'd arrived. He couldn't be involved in Edmund's murder. Still, closed minds created incorrect solutions.

Lord Faversham returned with a small wooden box in his hands. He opened it to reveal a few more antiquated pieces, mainly Roman.

"They're rather fun, don't you think?" he asked.

"I didn't know you had an interest in collecting." I inspected the items.

"I dabble. It passes the time, and you find some fascinating pieces."

"You're particularly interested in the Roman era? Or would you have bought items smuggled through the tunnels, too?"

"It depends on what they were," Lord Faversham said. "I don't have a fancy for a particular era, just when something takes my eye. I wouldn't have bought these, but Edmund said he'd run into a spot of trouble with his finances and offered them to me for a decent price."

"Edmund held down a respectable job," Jacob said. "Surely he shouldn't have had concerns about money."

"He spent a fair amount on ensuring the tunnels were safe," Lord Faversham replied, closing the wooden box and setting it on the table. "There was a collapse when he was down there one evening, so he got a few men in, and they shored it up. He was determined to find the treasure he believed his family hid."

"It can't be cheap shoring up an underground tunnel," Jacob said. "Did the money you gave him cover the work required?"

"Most of it, I believe," Lord Faversham said. "He wouldn't have needed to sell anything to me, but when

Samuel cut him off, he had no option but to look elsewhere."

"Samuel?" I asked.

"Samuel Drake," Lord Faversham said. "He runs the antique shop in town. I don't know the ins and outs, but they had a falling out. Before that, Samuel provided funding to support Edmund's endeavours. I imagine they had a financial arrangement about splitting any profits. Samuel bet on him, but perhaps he realised there was no treasure to be had."

"I wonder if the police have spoken to Samuel," I said to Jacob. "They must know of the connection between the men."

"Bishop hasn't mentioned it," he replied.

"It may not be public knowledge," Lord Faversham said. "It was a gentleman's agreement—done over a handshake—so there wouldn't be paperwork. That's what Edmund said, anyway. He was disappointed when Samuel lost interest. That was why I stepped in and bought some of his bits. He was so down at the mouth about the possibility of stopping."

"Did you believe Edmund would uncover a fortune hidden in the tunnels?" I asked.

"Honestly, no. But he was always excited about some new find or other," Lord Faversham said. "Any family with long established roots in this town is aware of what came through those tunnels. I must confess, there are bottles of wine in my cellar that arrived through that route. As for a fortune in gold and jewels, I'm not so sure. It's a wonderful legend, though. And Edmund recently discovered something that had him bright-eyed and bushy tailed."

"What did he find?" I asked.

"He wouldn't tell me," Lord Faversham said, "but he was eager to get back to the tunnels. He even said his day job was hampering progress. I suggested he become a full-time treasure hunter, and he actually considered it!"

"I didn't realise you were so close to Edmund," I said.

"We passed the time when we met in the Green Man," Lord Faversham said. "I always enjoyed hearing about his adventures. He'd even come through from the tunnel into the pub for a drink and get chased out by your landlord for leaving muddy footprints everywhere."

"Did you happen to see Edmund arrive in the pub on the night he died?" I asked.

"No! The first time I saw him was when we entered the snug. Before that, I'd just bought a round of drinks for the crew of the Merry Widow. They were celebrating a bumper catch and promised to send me a crate of something special."

That would be simple information to check. Although if I hadn't been with Lord Faversham when discovering Edmund's body, I'd be tempted to question him more about his alibi. I was glad I didn't have to. I didn't want to jeopardise the opportunity to expand our work with abandoned animals. But Edmund's connection to Samuel Drake intrigued me, and I'd speak to him shortly.

"Shall we raise a glass again? To celebrate our new endeavour together?" Lord Faversham asked.

"I'd be glad to. Provided you have no more doubts as to our abilities," I said.

"My dear lady, even if I had doubts, you'd whisk them away with a clever word. I must confess, I was most put out when you hung up on me mid-conversation, but I understand your passion for helping animals in need. And when I saw those sad little creatures you'd rescued from the O'Rourke family clutches, I allowed my emotions to override my sensibilities."

"The two can comfortably coexist," I said. "I have an immense fondness for animals, but we must be practical with their care. We have the perfect arrangement. The animals will want for nothing, and we won't get in your way."

"I shall visit regularly and jolly well get in your way," Lord Faversham said with a chuckle. "And I may muck in myself and help now and again."

"Cheers to that," Jacob said. "And here's to a successful shelter for the dogs in Kent."

We raised our glasses and celebrated our new adventure. It was an exciting time. If only the inconvenience of a body in my pub's snug wasn't distracting me, life would be almost perfect. But I was a capable multitasker.

After finishing our drinks, shaking hands with Lord Faversham, and agreeing with him on a timetable for signing the paperwork to make our arrangement formal, we left his manor house.

We took a leisurely walk back to the stables, and after checking on Molly, happy to see she was hard at work, and the rest of the volunteers were on their way, I collected Benji and we climbed into the car and returned to town.

Jacob glanced at me. "I know what you're thinking."

"That I'm happy we finally have a place for unwanted dogs in this county?"

"Well, yes, that. But you want to speak to Samuel, don't you?"

"Of course I do. This is a new suspect. If Edmund and Samuel's business deal went wrong, there could have been bad blood between the men."

"I should insist you return to your lodgings and rest," Jacob said.

"But you know it would be a waste of breath," I replied. "It won't take me long to speak to Samuel and find out what he knew about Edmund. What if they argued about their arrangement? Or Edmund promised Samuel something and didn't deliver? Samuel was providing financial support with the expectation of receiving a fortune. If Edmund pulled the wool over his eyes, he may not have taken it well."

"You could relay the information to Bishop, and he'd send an officer to ask the same questions," Jacob said.

"It'll take five minutes. And then I'll rest."

"You never rest."

"I do! When essential. Although I'll never understand the role of being a lady of leisure or a housewife."

"You'd never be content as a housewife, ironing my shirts and making my dinners. Although many women would adore that role," Jacob said, a smile tracing across his lips.

I shuddered. "If you left me in charge of the household, your dinners would be burned or undercooked. And as for the ironing, I hope you like the singed look."

Jacob laughed out loud. "I'm happy to be an independent chap. I don't want to risk you giving me food poisoning."

"How dare you!" I gasped in mock outrage. "I would only poison you with an undercooked fillet a few times a year at the most. Your constitution would toughen up if you had me in charge in the kitchen."

"We'll get someone in for the meals," Jacob said.

"Someone in where?"

"When we're married." He glanced at me. "Don't look so shocked. That's the way things are going, aren't they?"

I took a moment to compose myself, clutching my handbag a little tighter. We were heading in that direction, and I was happy about it. It was a slow, steady pace as I explored my connection with Jacob. He was always there, steadfast and firm, no matter what predicament I got myself into.

"Perhaps we should do it while we're in Faversham," I said. "It's a pleasant enough town."

"Veronica! You're the epitome of practicality, but when we marry, I want our friends and family to attend. It'll be a cause for celebration, not a task to tick off your list."

"That sounds expensive," I said.

"We'll pick one of your prettiest pubs, get married in the local church, and have fish and chips afterwards in the pub."

"I'd rather pie and mash," I said.

Jacob slowed the car and pulled over to the side of the road. "Then pie and mash it is. Here's the antique shop. Would you like me to come with you?"

"I know how busy you are at the office. You get to work, and I'll have a friendly chat with Samuel and see what secrets he reveals." I stepped out of the car, Benji joining me.

Gosh! All this talk of marriage could quite unnerve a woman if she didn't have a steely constitution and an iron will not to become distracted by such a complication.

I took a deep breath and focused on the task at hand. The antique shop had a faded green frontage. Although the paint was peeling in places, the window display was attractive enough. Silver platters and matching goblets, an array of gleaming rings arranged neatly on a velvet-lined shelf.

I headed inside and almost walked into a customer who was dashing out.

The pretty blonde pulled up short, but we were so close to colliding, I caught a whiff of her perfume. "Oh, my goodness!"

"My apologies. My mind was elsewhere," I said.

Her expression softened. "As was mine. And Mr Drake has been most unhelpful. I wouldn't waste your time if I were you."

"Is he unfriendly?" I peered over her shoulder.

"Abrupt. You would think he wasn't interested in selling me any jewellery. Good day to you." The young woman hurried away, her heeled boots clipping along like a spirited mare.

When I finally stepped inside the shop, I discovered I was the only patron. I browsed for a moment, pretending interest in a slightly tarnished pocket watch, until a short man with broad shoulders and a neat, dark beard stepped out from the back room.

He smiled warmly. "Good day, madam. Is there something in particular you're searching for?"

I introduced myself and Benji. "I'm looking for information if you have a moment to talk. Have you heard that Edmund Blackwood was recently found dead in the Green Man?"

The only sign of surprise on Samuel's face was a slight twitch of one eyebrow. "Indeed, I have. Terrible business."

"My family owns the Green Man," I said. "You may have noticed the name Vale above the door."

"That's you? How remarkable."

"Perhaps to some. Since Edmund died on my premises, I'm interested in learning what happened."

Samuel inclined his head. "Naturally. But why ask me about him?"

I held his gaze. "Because you were in business together."

He hesitated just a beat before replying. "What have you heard?"

"That Edmund was obsessed with finding the Blackwood treasure. He came to you with a proposal to work together."

Samuel's nostrils flared. "You are well informed."

"I'm friendly with Lord Faversham. He's a well-connected chap." I didn't like to name drop, but sometimes, it encouraged a more open conversation.

"Goodness! You are a surprising lady. And I feel honoured if Lord Faversham speaks of my work."

"He only had good things to say." I smiled as sweetly as I could muster. "I'd be interested in your arrangement with Edmund."

"It was all aboveboard, and the terms were generous. You can tell Lord Faversham that. I'm an honest chap to do business with."

"Naturally, I will. Please, go on."

Samuel stood upright with his chest puffed. "I had my doubts Edmund would ever deliver on his promises, but I was happy to extend him a small investment."

"Did Edmund ever bring any items into your shop to sell?"

"A few coins and some interesting tools, which I sold, but nothing on the scale we'd discussed. I knew it was a wild shot to expect him to uncover chests full of gold coins, but there was always hope. If he'd succeeded, it would've been the making of both of us."

"Does your business not prosper?" I glanced around the interior. While the window offered a charming glimpse, the rest of the shop was dimly lit, the items lacking appeal.

"Antiques are in the blood," he said. "This has been a family business for three generations. I was proud to take it over."

"You must be doing well if you were happy to extend financing to Edmund's venture."

"I get by," he said simply.

"But not well enough to keep the investment going," I said. "Perhaps you thought the treasure hunting was a waste of resources. Or maybe..." I let the suggestion hang. "You didn't trust Edmund."

"Why would I ever doubt Edmund's word?" Samuel's gaze narrowed slightly.

"Did you become concerned he'd discovered the treasure and wasn't sharing it with you?" I asked. "He might have realised how much money he could make on his own, so he cut you out of the deal. Some may say that's a motive for ending a man's life."

Samuel shook his head. "As I said, my business is flourishing. I don't need such outlandish measures to make my fortune. I did it more for my amusement than anything else. Besides, our financial arrangement was small. I provided Edmund with funds for tools, not a wage."

"You only worked with him because it amused you?"

Samuel tutted. "We shared an interest in the past. I'm an honest chap. All legit."

"Which means you won't mind me enquiring as to your whereabouts on the night of Edmund's death," I said.

A smug smile crossed Samuel's face. "I was dining with a wealthy American client. You may telephone the restaurant where I made the reservation. The lobster was sublime."

After noting down the restaurant's name, I gave him a polite nod. His motive was plausible, and until I confirmed his alibi, Samuel Blake remained on my list of suspects.

"I am sorry Edmund is dead, but I can help you no further." He edged towards the back room. "If you'll excuse me, I have an appointment with a dealer."

I took one last look around the shop before stepping onto the pavement. For a business that was supposedly flourishing, there were few treasures to be seen. Most of the stock was uninspiring, dusty, and looked like it had sat untouched for years.

If Samuel was making money, I doubted it was from selling these antiques.

# Chapter 15

I finished my third cup of coffee, my nerves jangling from all the stimulation. I longed to stretch my legs and take a long walk with Benji, but my priority was figuring out exactly what Samuel Drake was up to.

I'd settled myself at a window table in the small, low-ceilinged café situated opposite the antique shop. The décor was faded, and the drinks weren't particularly hot, but it was cheap, and the owner hadn't minded me conducting my stakeout at a table, provided I kept buying drinks. He'd even allowed Benji to sneak in under the table, so I had everything I needed to enact my plan.

The only time I'd left the café was to telephone Jacob and ask him to meet me for dinner. He was due any moment, and I had plenty to tell him.

"Is there anything else I can get for you?" The man who ran the café single-handedly walked to the table and took away my empty cup.

"I'll be ordering an evening meal soon," I said. "What can you recommend?"

"The pie's not bad. I buy them from the local market. We've got fish, too."

"Leave the menu, and I'll take a look."

He was happy to do so and ambled away.

A moment later, Jacob appeared. He stepped through the door and looked around, not seeming pleased by his surroundings. I gestured him over to the table, and he kissed my cheek before taking a seat, giving Benji's head a quick rub as he did so.

"When you said you wanted to go for dinner, I thought it would be a little more romantic than this." Jacob peered at the gloomy interior of the small, shabby dining establishment.

I arched an eyebrow at him. "We aren't here for romance. We're here to monitor a murder suspect. This location is perfect to watch what's going on at the antique shop."

"So much for resting if you've been here most of the day," Jacob said.

"I have been sitting all day. What is that if not rest?"

Jacob eyed the curled paper menu. "What have you learned?"

"Samuel Drake attempts to come across as a gentleman of means, but his business is a front. And I don't trust a word that comes out of his mouth."

"Because..."

"Other than a disgruntled young woman who was in the shop when I arrived, he hasn't received a single customer all day."

Jacob lowered the menu and peered across the street. "Could he be smuggling in illegal goods? Selling them elsewhere?"

"He's doing something to earn a crust. Not antiques. No one has gone through that door. Samuel is hiding something. He needs to be top of the suspect list."

"Maybe not. I had a telephone call from Bishop just before leaving," Jacob said. "He's spoken to one of the local beat coppers. They think Edmund's murder is connected to trouble at the bank where he worked."

"Goodness. What kind of trouble?"

"There was an anonymous tip-off that claimed someone was stealing from the bank. Not large amounts but enough to get noticed when there was an audit. An audit Edmund oversaw."

"Edmund uncovered the theft?" I asked.

"We'll never know for certain," Jacob said. "Although there are policemen searching the bank to see if he left behind evidence of his concerns. Maybe a list of employees he had doubts about."

"That would be a solid motive for wanting him dead," I said. "If Edmund discovered a member of staff slipping a few notes into their pockets, they'd want to silence him. It would end their career and put them in prison."

"That's where the police are focusing their efforts," Jacob said. "And I think they're on to something."

"What about Samuel?" I jabbed a finger at the grimy window. "I can confirm he's not selling antiques from that shop."

"Perhaps it's a slow day."

The café owner wandered over to take our order. "What will it be?"

"Before we order, do you know much about the antique shop?" I asked.

"Such as it is," the man said. "I don't know how Mr Drake keeps the place going. You never know whether it'll be open. I asked him about it once, and he said he's often away on business, looking for stock, but he never comes back with much."

"Does he have regular customers who buy from him?"

"Not that I've noticed."

"His family has run that shop for a long time, haven't they?"

"I can't say as they have," the café owner replied.

"Samuel said antiques were in his blood and they'd had the shop for generations."

The café owner pursed his lips. "That's odd. I've been here ten years, but I'm sure that was a tobacconist shop when I moved here. I suppose his family could have moved or opened a second shop." He nodded at the menu. "Have you decided yet?"

We both ordered meat pie, mashed potatoes, peas, and a round of drinks. I opted for something without caffeine.

The café owner ambled off into the kitchen to dish up our dinner.

"If the antique shop is a front for illegal activities," I said, "perhaps Edmund found out and confronted Samuel. He was worried Samuel would cheat him. Or he was concerned that any finds he discovered would be sold on the black market."

"Or Edmund discovered what Samuel was really up to and wanted a cut," Jacob said. "If Samuel is smuggling in something illegal and selling it under the counter, he wouldn't have wanted Edmund getting in the way."

"Samuel provided me with his alibi for the night of Edmund's murder." I stood and pushed back my chair.

"You want to check it now?" Jacob asked. "What about our dinner?"

"I won't be long. I need to make a telephone call. Sit tight with Benji, and I'll be back in a jiffy." I dashed off, located the nearest telephone booth, and pulled out the piece of paper where I'd jotted the restaurant's name. I contacted the operator to get the connection.

A few moments later, a smooth-voiced man answered. "Good evening. The Lobster Pot. How may I assist you?"

"I'd like to check a reservation I made for my employer, Samuel Drake." I confirmed the date of the dinner and waited a moment, listening as pages rustled.

"Here it is, madam. I can confirm a reservation for that evening was booked for five o'clock."

"Wonderful. Could you confirm what time Mr Drake and his companion left the restaurant?"

"I'm sorry. I wasn't working that evening. We reserve dining slots for three hours if that's any help, so they could have been here until at least eight o'clock."

"Thank you. I appreciate your time." I said my goodbyes and hung up.

Samuel hadn't lied about where he was that evening, but I still didn't trust the man.

I hurried back to the café to find our food being set down on the table.

"Did you learn anything useful?" Jacob prodded a rather pale-looking meat pie with his fork.

"Samuel was at dinner with someone on the night Edmund died," I said. "Perhaps we should follow the theory about the crooked teller. I'll speak to Colin and see if any bank staff were in the Green Man that night."

Jacob rested his hand gently on top of mine. "Before you dash off again, you need to eat."

"I wasn't planning on dashing anywhere. I'm looking forward to my meal." I absolutely had been. Once I had a bee in my bonnet, I couldn't relax.

"Veronica, it'll do you no good to keep pushing yourself. You were recently injured, and you've barely rested since then."

"I rested all night." I stabbed at my pie with more force than necessary. "Besides, a small bump to the head won't slow me."

Jacob looked at me steadily. "Without Ruby watching over you, you're not taking the best care of yourself."

"Ruby? Who needs her?"

"You do. She may be flippant at times, but she has a heart of gold, and she always knows how best to take care of you and ensure you don't do too many foolish things."

My appetite dimmed. I set down my fork and looked away from the plate.

"Tell me what's wrong between the two of you," Jacob said gently. "It must be something serious. You've never spent this much time apart."

I glanced at Jacob. He was my companion. And if his comments about marriage in the future came true, there should be no secrets between us.

He nodded, encouraging me to share.

"As you know, Ruby suddenly went missing. At first, I was terribly concerned about her safety. Sergeant Matthers even checked the morgues to see if any bodies had been brought in."

"Veronica! I had no idea you were that concerned about her."

"I was covering all eventualities. I hoped, as everyone else did, that she'd found herself a nice young man who'd swept her off on a whirlwind adventure. But then I learned the truth."

Jacob's brow furrowed. "Which is?"

"Ruby is pregnant."

Jacob's eyebrows shot up. "When did you meet to discover that?"

"We haven't met."

"Then how do you know she is expecting a child?

"I saw her without her knowing," I said. "She's colluding with Lady M. She must have convinced her to fake concern about her whereabouts to put me off the scent. Lady M knows exactly what's going on with Ruby because Ruby is living with her."

"My word. And the father? Is he living with Lady M too?"

"Unknown to me," I said. "It could be that dreadful Italian chap Ruby almost married. They were fond of each other. Passionate, too. But with Ruby's free spirit, she may have met someone else who took her fancy and lost her sensibilities."

Jacob was quiet for a moment as he ate a bite of his dinner. "What are you doing here when Ruby is in such a predicament?"

"Ruby has landed firmly on her feet," I said with a sniff. "She's taken up residence with Lady M. She'll want for nothing."

"She's your best friend. And Ruby will need help. We know times are changing, but they're slow to fully evolve. An unmarried pregnant woman is a source of shame for many. You should be by her side."

"That's impossible. Ruby lied to me." I looked away, the words catching slightly in my throat. "She vanished without a proper word about where she was going. And now she's concealing the pregnancy and involving others in her deceit." Those others not being me. It was a bitter blow to a friendship I'd considered unbreakable.

"Ruby must be terrified," Jacob said. "And you are the best of friends, so she'll be afraid of your judgement."

"If we are best friends, she'd know I wouldn't judge her. I'd fix everything."

Jacob sighed softly. "Hear your own words. That might be the exact opposite of what Ruby wants. She's likely got a dozen possibilities running through her head, deciding what to do about this pregnancy."

This man never failed to surprise me. He knew me so well. "That concern had crossed my mind. Ruby won't want me swooping in, taking control and dictating things. That's why she's hiding. That doesn't mean it hurts any less."

Jacob nodded. "She needs time to figure it out for herself. To fix things herself."

I grabbed my fork and stabbed it into the pie several times, letting out a plume of steam. "It unsettles me that you know my mind better than I do."

"It should be a comfort."

I glanced up at him. "It is. And I don't mean to snap at you. I'm more upset than I want anyone to know. I feel as if I've lost Ruby."

"Not lost. Not with a friendship so strong." Jacob offered a small smile. "Ruby still adores you. She wants you in her life, but she's not sure how to manage that, given her new situation."

I gulped against the lump rising in my throat. "I miss her dreadfully. She makes everything lighter. Joy sparkles out of her. Without her, I feel dreadfully dowdy."

"I never see you as dowdy," Jacob said. "But I think it's time you reached out. Tell her you know she's staying with Lady M and that you're here if she needs anything. Remind her you're still her friend and you only want what's best for her."

"She... she wrote to me recently," I said. "It was sent to my London address. My mother tried to read the letter to me, but I wouldn't hear it. Perhaps I was too hasty."

"Write back to Ruby. You'll figure things out. If she plans on keeping the child, she'll need help. Perhaps she'll even ask you to be the child's godparent."

I grimaced and scooped up a forkful of mashed potatoes. "I'm terrible with infants. Present me with a basket of adorable puppies and I'm in my element. But a newborn child? Perish the thought."

Jacob chuckled. "Having a child in your life could open up all kinds of possibilities."

I huffed out a breath and stabbed a pea. "I'd much rather have a basket full of puppies."

# Chapter 16

"Thank you for seeing me at such short notice." I smiled politely as I sat at one of four desks in the small bank of Hitchcock and Halls. Benji wasn't with me, but in Colin's capable and treat-heavy hands.

"It's my pleasure, Mrs Vale." The man who sat opposite me, William Wilcocks, assistant bank manager, smoothed a hand down his tie. "We welcome all enquiries from potential customers and always find time for them. Will your husband not be joining us?"

"He'll be here shortly. As I mentioned on the telephone this morning, we're considering expanding our business operations. We already have a base in Margate, but we have more work than we can handle, so we're considering opening additional offices."

William made a few notes on the pad in front of him. "I'm happy to hear your husband's business is a success. I don't believe you told me what line of work he is in."

I paused, my gaze shifting over his shoulder. Jacob's friend, Bishop, had just entered the bank with two uniformed officers accompanying him.

William noticed my distraction. "Oh, don't mind them. I assure you, this is a legitimate business." He gave a high-pitched laugh.

"It's somewhat alarming to see the police here," I said. "Is there trouble I need to be aware of?"

"No! No trouble. Let's move somewhere quieter," William offered. "I'll have my assistant make us tea, and we can talk uninterrupted in a private room."

"I would like that. I'm unused to discussing matters of business so publicly." And it would get me out of the way before Bishop caught me snooping. He'd said he'd welcome information on any leads I had, but I doubted he'd appreciate me stepping on too many uniformed toes and making the police appear slow and foolish.

William patted the back of my hand. "Say no more. We'll make ourselves comfortable, and you can tell me about your business ideas. Although, are you sure we shouldn't wait for your husband? Business matters can be complicated if you're used to more domestic endeavours."

I gritted my teeth but forced a sweet smile. "I'll manage until he arrives."

A few moments later, we were settled in a comfortably furnished, small office. The photographs on the walls were black-and-white images of the town, and the furnishings were neat and practical. A photograph of a pretty young woman sat on the desk. I recognised her as the lady I'd almost walked into when visiting Samuel's antique shop.

"Are those police officers here because of what happened to Edmund Blackwood?" I asked.

William's eyebrows lifted. "Oh! Well, yes, they are. Did you know Mr Blackwood?"

"A little. And I remember seeing you in the Green Man." I'd studied William and recognised him as the nervous chap who'd attempted to speak to Edmund and been given the brush-off.

"I thought your face looked familiar. My apologies for not recognising you," William said. "Since Edmund's departure under such sad circumstances, we've been at sixes and sevens."

"Yes, I imagine that is a strain," I said. "Did you report directly to him?"

William nodded. "I'm one of two assistant managers. I've been here the longest, so I have more seniority."

"I'm sorry for your loss," I said, noting not a jot of sadness from William.

"Thank you. Now, perhaps we could turn to your interest in business financing? Do you have premises in mind for the expansion?"

"If we could delay that topic a moment," I said. "I actually have a personal interest in what happened to Edmund."

William shifted in his seat. "I thought you said you weren't a resident of the town?"

"I'm not. But I have a business interest here," I said. "The Green Man."

William looked bemused. "The pub? What about it?"

"It belongs to my family," I said.

"Your father's concern?"

"My father is sadly no longer with us," I replied. "I look after the pub's day-to-day dealings."

"That's the business you're in?" William looked increasingly confused. "You want financing for a pub?"

"That side of my business interests is firmly in the black and doing marvellously," I said. "I have another arm of business. Private investigation."

He dropped his pen. "My, my. You are a busy lady, helping with your late father's pub and assisting your husband with investigations. You must have excellent shorthand and organisational skills."

"I have many skills. It never does one good to remain idle," I said sweetly. "If you're not learning, your mind withers."

"I... well. I suppose so." William fiddled with his pen. "This private investigation work has you looking into what happened to Mr Blackwood?"

"Edmund was discovered dead in the Green Man. I want to find out why someone thought it acceptable to do such a terrible thing under my roof."

William opened his mouth and drew in a breath, glancing around the room with bewilderment. "Yes! Naturally. That makes sense. But surely you can't get enjoyment from such a task?"

"I can't imagine why anyone would be unhappy about solving an injustice," I said. "It's one reason I opened the business in Margate."

"You opened it? I thought you said your husband was the mastermind behind that plan. I assumed you were his secretary."

"I am a thoroughly modern woman."

William's nose wrinkled, and he touched the photograph of the woman on his desk. "Yes, well, be that as it may, I'm not sure I approve. I'm aware of a shift in the way things are. Since the Great War ended, women have become outspoken and desirous of different things."

"People must change and grow. Don't you agree?" My smile felt too sharp as I glared at William.

"I can't see the problem with how things were before the war. I like tradition. The natural order. A stay-at-home wife is the best kind of wife. Too many ambitions lead to bad decisions." William looked at the photograph.

"Is that your wife?" I spoke through gritted teeth.

"Not yet, but soon. Elizabeth abides by tradition. She has the most charming demeanour."

It was almost beyond me to bite my tongue. I wanted to unleash my fury on this outdated chap, but that would get me nowhere with my investigation. So, I swallowed my pride, extracted a handkerchief from my handbag, and dabbed it delicately against my nose.

"I've found it incredibly overwhelming. Finding a man almost dead in the pub and being unable to save him haunts me."

William squirmed in his seat at the sight of my distress. "Goodness! You found Mr Blackwood's body?"

"Indeed, I did. I thought everyone was aware of that. It's all I've heard people talk about. They gossip about tragedy as if it were a sale at the local dress shop."

William leaned forward in his seat, his gaze intent. "When you found Mr Blackwood, what was it like?"

I hid my surprise at his blunt questioning by using my handkerchief to dab imaginary tears from the corners of my eyes. "An utter shock. I walked into the snug, and there he was on the floor, taking his last breaths."

"Did he say anything to you?"

"He was trying to talk. I'm sure he had information as to his killer."

"But he didn't tell you who hit him, did he?"

"Sadly not. Which must be why the police are here, to find out everything about Edmund," I said.

"I understand now why you're so fascinated by this terrible event," William said. "You should see the doctor to get something for your nerves. My mother suffers dreadfully with her nerves, but she gets a powder from the doctor. It does wonders for her."

"My sleep has suffered," I said, with as demure an air as I could muster.

William set down his pen, no longer interested in the matter of business. "Was there any evidence in the snug to suggest who did this to Mr Blackwood?"

I looked at William from beneath lowered lashes. This gentleman had gone from attempting to change the subject away from murder to being fascinated by it. Why was that? Was he concerned he'd left a clue that implicated him?

"I'm sure the police found useful evidence," I said. "They've been speaking to several individuals they're interested in regarding this callous act."

"Who are they most interested in?" William almost whispered his question, unaware of how anxious he appeared.

I stifled a fake sob. "I don't want to think about it, but I can't help myself. I must know what happened. And I feel partly responsible. I should never have given Edmund access to the snug to conduct his business.

Then he wouldn't have been there, in full view of a cold-blooded killer who wanted him gone."

William's expression softened as he believed my helpless lady act. "The police around here do a sterling job. They'll find out who did this. Don't distress yourself."

"I'm sure you're right," I said. "Have they spoken to you yet?"

He nodded. "They interviewed everyone at the bank. The police needed a full picture of Mr Blackwood's life to learn if there was anyone who wanted to cause him trouble."

"Did anyone come to your mind?" I asked. "Was Edmund an unkind employer?"

"He was a reasonable man. Well-respected." William shook himself and shuffled the papers in front of him. "We should get back to looking at your business financing."

I persisted. "Where were you when you heard the dreadful news?"

"Here! The police came to the bank the morning after Mr Blackwood died. They gathered us together and told us what had happened."

"Did they ask for your alibi?"

"They asked us all that question," William said. "I understand why they needed to know, but it felt jolly uncomfortable being put on the spot like that. I almost felt guilty, even though I'd done nothing wrong."

I nodded along, encouraging him to continue. He remained silent and shuffled the papers again.

I decided to share information, hoping to loosen his tongue. Well, that and make him concerned I'd walk away from wanting to do business with a bank I didn't consider trustworthy.

"I've heard a rumour there were problems at this bank that involved Edmund," I said.

"No problems. This is a most excellent institution," William said. "I'm proud to work here."

"I'm sure the rumours don't involve you," I continued, "but someone told me money had gone missing."

William sucked in a sharp breath. "Who has been spreading such disgraceful misinformation?"

"It's come up more than once in conversation. Is it true?" I hoped my expression mirrored my shocked tone. "I'm unsure if I could enter into an agreement with a bank where they're unable to manage money safely."

William's expression flashed from irritated to concerned before smoothing out. "I always stress honesty in business dealings, so I will be frank with you. Before Mr Blackwood died, a recent audit discovered small irregularities."

"Someone is stealing from the bank?" I clutched my handbag. "I should go elsewhere. Are there other banks in Faversham where the staff are honest?"

"No! There's no need. We are a highly regarded institution," William said with undue haste. "But rumours spread quickly when wicked deeds are done. We need to squash this one."

"I am the soul of discretion. What can you tell me so I know this bank is trustworthy?"

William regarded me coolly, but the gleam of perspiration on his brow revealed his genuine anxiety. "The Bank of England's regulatory arm conducted an audit. It's a routine practice banks go through to ensure everything is shipshape. Mr Blackwood was fully involved, and he recruited his most trusted assistants to help."

"You are one such assistant?"

"Naturally. I was even here on the night of Mr Blackwood's death, working late to finish the paperwork he should have completed for the audit."

"Why didn't he do it?"

William pressed his lips together. "You're likely aware that Mr Blackwood had an unusual passion outside of banking."

"I do! That was why he was interested in the Green Man," I said. "He could access an old smuggling tunnel from my cellar."

"Mr Blackwood's hobby interfered with his work," William said. "He would leave early to get to the tunnel before dark. I never complained, but over time, he shifted more of his work onto me. I was running this bank in the last few months of Mr Blackwood's life. The man was obsessed with those tunnels."

"I understand Edmund invested money into his hobby," I said.

William's gaze took on a conspiratorial gleam. "Yes! And although this bank pays fairly, I'm not sure it paid enough for Mr Blackwood to finance everything he needed to do."

I faked a startled gasp. "Do you mean to say Edmund was stealing from the bank?"

William raised a hand. "I don't like to speak ill of the dead, but I was worried he was the source of the irregularities. I have prepared a report outlining my concerns."

I sat back in my seat. Since Samuel Drake had removed his financial support from Edmund's excavation activities, he'd have needed to look elsewhere. Would Edmund have risked stealing from the bank to finance his desire to find the missing treasure?

"Now Mr Blackwood is no longer with us, the irregularities will vanish," William said decisively. "Mrs Vale, you can trust this bank. We're a steadfast institution. Why don't you look at this financing example, assuming you can make sense of the figures?"

I half-heartedly perused the figures William set out for me, but my mind was elsewhere. I was missing a clue, but what was it?

"You're welcome to look at the information for as long as you desire, but I'll need your husband to sign the paperwork," William said. "Bring him with you next time you make an appointment. The interest rates and repayment terms are complex when you're unfamiliar with financing."

Now I had the information I needed, I dropped my disguise. "I'm happy to say I'm unmarried."

William made a startled choking sound. "Unmarried? What are you doing here? We don't provide financing to unmarried women."

"Then your bank is missing a magnificent opportunity." I stood and collected my handbag. "And I assure you, if I need money, I invest from my own healthy savings."

"Then what in all heavens have you been doing here? Why all the questions about Mr Blackwood? What is going on?"

A knock on the door saved me from answering the barrage of questions. Bishop opened it a second later. Drat. Caught snooping. I offered him an apologetic smile.

"I'm sorry for interrupting," he said. "Miss Vale, would you mind if I had a word?"

# Chapter 17

Bishop took me to a quiet area in the bank to ensure privacy.

"I assume you're here because of Edmund?" he asked.

"I decided to continue investigating independently. The police are moving too slowly for my liking. Leads are growing cold."

He choked out a laugh. "Steady on! We're doing our best. And I don't know this area well, so I have fewer contacts to draw upon."

"Is the man in charge of the local police inefficient?" I asked. "The chap in London rarely knows what day of the week it is until he's reminded, and even then, he gets in a fluster."

"We don't have that issue. The Kent chief is a good sort and runs a respectable team."

"That's reassuring. But even so, I must get to the bottom of what happened to Edmund. You'd do the same if you found a body in your place of work."

"Veronica, go easy on me," Bishop said. "Jacob has told me you're whip-smart and stand for no nonsense, but I'll be the one who gets hauled over the coals if you're caught snooping and our names become associated."

"If that unlikely event happens, I'll pretend I've never met you before," I said. "Does that make you feel better?"

"Hardly! My superior isn't stupid. He'll figure things out. I'm happy to have your input, but you must be more discreet."

I sighed softly. "My apologies for stomping on your toes. I'm here to help."

"Which is why I'm not arresting you for interfering in police matters," he said. "And I do appreciate any input. I'm not underselling the dire situation we have here."

"I didn't realise things were so grim."

Bishop glanced over his shoulder. "A few months ago, several officers were let go because they got caught taking backhanders. The men up top have been slow to recruit, and there are still rumours a few higher-ups might also be on the take. Everyone's jumpy."

"That sounds unpleasant," I said. "But it's all the more reason to pull on the assets you have. Jacob and I are here to step into the breach. I'll hide nothing from you if you're open with me."

"Thank you. Just, please, do so more discreetly. I like my job. I don't want to lose it."

"Understood. Since we're here, we may as well share notes," I said. "Do you believe there are shady goings-on at the bank?"

"It looks likely. There's money missing," Bishop said. "Only small amounts taken over six months, but it adds up."

"My conversation with William was illuminating as to who that person may be."

"What did you uncover?"

"At first, I wondered if it was William. He's a nervous sort. And I was in the Green Man when he confronted Edmund. He wanted to talk about something urgent. Edmund dismissed him, but William wasn't happy. Perhaps it was to do with the missing money."

"You now have doubts?"

"William pointed the finger at Edmund as the thief," I said. "According to him, Edmund neglected his duties here to obsess over searching for his missing family fortune. He gave William more responsibility in the bank, which led to him uncovering the irregularities."

"And you think Edmund hadn't covered his tracks as well as he thought?" Bishop asked.

"Or perhaps William was smarter than he realised and saw through Edmund's attempt at a cover-up," I said. "William confronted Edmund, and a fight ensued. If both men were regulars at the Green Man, no one would have noticed them coming and going. William would have known Edmund used the pub as his base and snuck in to deal with him."

"I've interviewed William twice," Bishop said. "He appears honest."

"When we spoke, he appeared nervous," I said. "If he's not hiding something to do with the irregularities, there's another matter he's concealing."

Bishop smiled. "William is nervous because he's about to propose."

"Oh, that poor woman," I murmured. "Elizabeth has a world of disappointment about to rain down on that pretty head of hers."

"Why ever do you say that?"

"William was disparaging of my business endeavours," I said. "He told me exactly what he wants out of a woman. He said his lady friend is cut from an old-fashioned cloth. It's my idea of a nightmare."

Bishop chuckled. "Not everyone is as progressive as you, Veronica."

"They should be. Still, whatever makes a person happy, so long as it does no one any harm," I said. "Although I imagine the gleam of a traditional home life will tarnish when Elizabeth sees everything she's missing, and William won't bend to her will."

"Or they simply have different values to you and will be happy together."

I snitched my nose, not liking the thought that I might be incorrect.

"I suppose it'll soon be you and Jacob," Bishop said.

"Doing each other harm?" I asked innocently, knowing what he alluded to.

"Getting married! You've been together for some time, I believe. Jacob spoke of you before you made your acquaintance formal."

"Oh, we have little time for such formalities. Perhaps when we're both retired and wondering what to do with ourselves, we'll wander up the aisle and set things right by the eyes of traditional society."

Bishop stared at me with his mouth open and then laughed again. "As you said, whatever makes you happy. But for now, keep your nose clean and your head down, so I don't get in trouble. We're making progress, but if my superior figures out you're involved, there'll be hell to pay, and I could do without that."

"I'll be discreet, but I intend to keep asking questions."

Bishop pursed his lips then shrugged. "I suppose that's all I can ask."

We said our goodbyes, and Bishop walked back to join his colleagues. I paused when I noticed a security guard standing by the door.

"This is all rather exciting, don't you think?" I asked.

"I'm not sure I'd call the police snooping about exciting," he said.

"Missing money is always a scandal," I said. "I was just speaking to the assistant manager, William, about such a thing."

The security guard looked a trifle startled. "Were you, indeed?"

"Yes! And Edmund. Poor Edmund, losing his life. So sad."

"It's been a busy week." The security guard opened the door for me.

I stayed where I was. "William said he was working here that night. The night Edmund died. I don't suppose you saw him, did you?"

The security guard's face wrinkled as he processed my question. "I worked that evening. I prefer the late shift. It's quiet. You don't get people asking questions."

I ignored the dig. "That must be wonderfully refreshing. Idle chatter is such a chore. So, William. He was here?"

When the guard realised I intended to prattle and annoy, he sighed. "The men in suits are working all hours on this audit to ensure the paperwork is filed. Mr Wilcocks worked until ten p.m. that night. He was yawning as he left, saying he was too tired to even eat dinner."

"It's good to see a man so dedicated to his work. Enjoy the rest of your day." I hurried out into the bright morning.

That was one suspect in the clear, so I'd achieved something. I deserved a reward after this adventure, and I knew exactly where to get it.

---

After sleuthing at the bank, I'd spent a few hours on the telephone catching up with Jacob, who was busy dealing with cases at our Margate office. I assured him I'd take it easy for the rest of the day, which fitted perfectly into my plan.

I'd hopped on the train with Benji and we'd taken an enjoyable ride through the Kent countryside to the charming town of Whitstable, known for its locally caught oysters and beautiful seaside.

The stunning setting wasn't my focus. I planned to dine at the Lobster Pot, where Samuel came with his client the night Edmund was murdered. I didn't trust Samuel, and although the restaurant said there was a booking for him on the evening of the murder, the server I'd talked to couldn't confirm he'd seen Samuel.

I was crossing two hurdles with one leap: treating myself to a delicious luncheon and checking a dubious alibi. And I'd booked under the name Veronica Drake and planned to present myself as Samuel's poorly put-upon wife, hoping to garner sympathy.

The smartly dressed attendant met me at the door, smiling politely. He looked at Benji and shook his head. "I'm sorry, madam, but we don't permit dogs inside. We have a wraparound veranda with marvellous views out to sea. It's a pleasant day, if you'd like to sit out there with him."

I willingly accepted the compromise, since I preferred the fresh air rather than a stuffy inside. We were seated at a small table with an excellent view of the sun sparkling across the water.

I took a few moments to peruse the menu before choosing a traditional plate of fishcake and chips. As the server finished taking my order, I caught his eye.

"Could I ask if you know Samuel Drake? He regularly eats here."

The server tucked away his notepad and nodded. "I know him."

I sighed and attempted to look pitiful. "Samuel is my husband, and I have... concerns about him."

"Concerns, madam?"

"Could you tell me who he last dined with? I believe it was on this date and time." I gave him the details.

The server looked puzzled. "I'm not sure I can help. Mr Drake is a regular customer. We value his patronage."

"You must, since he comes here so often," I said. "I'm concerned, you see. About another woman. It's dreadfully embarrassing, but it would set my mind at rest if you could let me know when he last dined here and who he brought with him."

The server's cheeks flushed scarlet. "Let me check the diary. I'll be back in a few minutes." He rushed away as if he were being chased by a rabid dog.

I gently adjusted my hair, making sure it concealed my healing head wound, and waited for my food and answers.

Five minutes later, a man in a dark suit and patterned tie marched to my table. "Mrs Drake?"

"Yes. Do we know each other?" I asked.

"If you are who you say you are, then we've never met." The man took the seat opposite me, his expression cold.

"I've not dined here before," I said, surprised by his unwelcoming tone. "But my husband uses this restaurant for entertaining."

"Samuel Drake is a most excellent customer. We value his patronage highly."

"As your server told me," I said. "And you are..."

"Mr Lewis. Restaurant manager. And you're... Mrs Drake?"

I narrowed my eyes. From the way this chap spoke, it was clear he didn't believe me. "I have questions about Mr Drake's whereabouts on a specific date."

"You haven't answered my question. Are you his wife?"

I drew in a slow breath. "You seem like a sensible man, Mr Lewis."

"Sensible enough to know which side my bread is buttered. I've been the restaurant's manager for ten years, and Mr Drake has been coming here all that time. He even supported us when times were hard during the Great War. We have a great loyalty towards him."

"Would you be so loyal if you knew Samuel was a prime suspect in a murder?"

Mr Lewis jerked back in his seat. "Murder, you say? How can that be? Here?"

"In Faversham, where he has his shop." I settled myself in my seat, prepared to reveal all.

"And what would you know about it? Because you're not Mr Drake's wife. I'm aware he's unattached."

I smiled faintly. "I may have deceived you about who I am, but only because I need information. I need to know if Samuel lied about his whereabouts on the night of this murder."

Mr Lewis spent a few seconds in silent contemplation. "My server mentioned a particular date and time. He brought out the booking calendar to show me. There is a reservation made under Mr Drake's name for the date in question. Isn't that evidence enough to show he had nothing to do with this murder?"

"Was Samuel actually here that night?" I asked. "I telephoned for the information, but the server I spoke to didn't work on the evening in question. Unless someone confirms Samuel dined here, his alibi is worthless."

Mr Lewis fell silent again. "May I ask why Mr Drake is a suspect?"

"He had financial dealings with the victim. There could have been trouble between them when he withdrew his money."

"Ah! Money or lack of it can make a chap do terrible things," Mr Lewis said.

"It sounds as if you have experience with such a thing."

"Not me. A family friend. It was a tricky situation."

"What kind of clients does Samuel bring here?" I asked.

"I really couldn't say. We value discretion."

"Not even a hint?"

Irritation flashed across Mr Lewis's face. "Mr Drake always asks for a private table at the back of the restaurant so they can talk freely. He tips generously and buys expensive wine, so I ensure they aren't disturbed."

"Does it always appear to be business meetings?" I asked.

He looked slightly uncomfortable and didn't answer right away. "I believe so."

"I'm aware Samuel is an important customer, but any information you overheard could be valuable to solving this heinous crime." I leaned forward. "Imagine the scandal if it's discovered you concealed the actions of a killer."

Mr Lewis stared out to sea for a long moment, and I allowed the silence to stretch between us, giving him the room he needed to wrestle with his conscience.

"I have overheard a few conversations. Not deliberately, of course, but several times, I caught snippets about consignments and suitable packaging to avoid detection," he said.

"That doesn't sound like the work of a reputable antique dealer," I said.

Mr Lewis adjusted his collar. "I've wondered about Samuel's business dealings. I even visited his antique shop in Faversham but found it closed and sadly lacking in appeal."

"Yes. My visit left me deeply unimpressed. Is there anything else you can tell me about Samuel?" I asked. "Anything that would cause you concern?"

Mr Lewis nodded, more as if he'd finalised an internal decision than an affirmation towards me. "The reservation you're enquiring about. Mr Drake never showed up, and neither did his dining companion."

"How interesting. Did anyone telephone to tell you not to hold the table?"

"No. I held it as long as possible, but eventually gave it to a young couple. Mr Drake never appeared."

I sat back in my seat, my excitement thrumming. I was right all along. We had our man.

# Chapter 18

"Your head wound looks much improved." Jacob leaned across the table in the Green Man and attempted to lift my hair and inspect my stitches.

I gently pushed his enquiring hands away. "Don't fuss. I heal quickly from any injury. Besides, it was a small scratch."

"There's no need to underplay things to appear the heroine," Jacob said. "Once this is over, I'm insisting we take a holiday."

"Will it be the seaside? I remember how well our last adventure turned out. And I suppose we'll include my mother again? That won't be much of a rest."

He chuckled. "Your mother sounds too busy with her new gentleman friend for a holiday. She telephoned the office again to update me on how things were going and to enquire as to your activities since you haven't returned her last three telephone calls."

"You're super for keeping her occupied. Although I hope you didn't tell her about my injury." I waved a hand at my head wound.

"If I had, she'd have been on the next train down from London," Jacob said. "Although perhaps I should tell her. You'd listen to her."

"Only when I can't avoid it," I said.

The pub doors opened, and Bishop strode in. He soon saw us and walked over, settling into a seat with an exhausted sigh, where a pint of ale waited for him.

"It seems we've all had a busy day of it," he said, after taking a sip of his ale. "I need this."

"Your interviews at the bank were fruitful?" I asked.

"Most likely as fruitful as yours. I saw you questioning the security guard after you should have left." Bishop arched an eyebrow at me.

"We were passing the time," I said. "It would have been rude not to engage in civil conversation."

"Veronica! We agreed to share all information. Don't say you've changed your mind."

"Indeed, I haven't."

"You questioned the security guard about where William was on the night of Edmund's murder," Bishop said.

Bishop was too thorough for his own good, although it meant he'd do a sterling job unpicking this murder.

"I was ensuring no stone was unturned. Security guards are ideal people to speak to. They're observant."

"I know! I've spoken to him more than once," Bishop said. "He's a reliable witness."

"His information helped me to rule William out as a suspect in Edmund's murder," I said. "I still favour Samuel Drake."

I'd updated Jacob about my fascinating discovery at the Lobster Pot earlier that day and quickly filled in

Bishop. When I finished, he sat back in his seat with a grunt, his forehead scrunched as if deep in thought.

"The notes we have about Samuel Drake show he was at dinner. A local officer confirmed it," Bishop said.

"Over the telephone?"

"I believe so. We don't have the manpower to send anyone on a jolly to Whitstable."

"Then it's fortunate you have female power. I met with the restaurant manager and discovered the information, but only after disclosing the serious nature of this crime. Samuel is a valued customer, but I convinced the manager that Samuel is less appealing when labelled a murderer."

"Steady on with making accusations," Bishop said. "Samuel is only a suspect. He hasn't been convicted of any crime."

"Only because he's too clever to be caught," I replied. "The man is pulling a deception through his antique shop. Maybe that deception led to something more serious."

Bishop shook his head. "I still prefer Charles Blackwood for this crime."

"It can't be him," I said. "He has an alibi."

"A gang of deceitful thugs," Bishop said. "Unreliable liars, who would sell their sister if the price was right."

"The O'Rourke family gains nothing from keeping Charles's secret," I said. "Once he's behind bars, they won't be able to recoup their debt. He's more use to them as a free man. You must question Samuel again. There's something about his arrangement that doesn't add up. There's nothing in that shop of value. That's your killer."

"Sorry, Veronica, but I disagree. We're bringing Charles in again," Bishop said. "We've done more investigating into his background and discovered extensive debts. The man was homeless and up to his eyeballs in loans, not just from the O'Rourke family. He has people chasing him from different criminal gangs."

"It's surprising he's still alive," Jacob said.

"He must have grown so desperate that he killed his brother, thinking he'd inherit his money," Bishop said. "Edmund had a well-paying career, so Charles knew there was money that would go to him. Edmund was unmarried, and Charles is the closest relative."

"It's a plausible theory." Jacob glanced at me.

"It's the one my superior prefers." Bishop finished his ale and yawned. "Now, if you'll excuse me, I need to get some shut-eye before it all starts again."

We said our goodbyes, and I watched him leave the pub.

"Don't be angry," Jacob said. "Bishop is only doing his job."

"It's foolish to focus on Charles as the killer," I said. "Samuel is equally plausible."

"If it comes to nothing with Charles, the police will turn their attention to Samuel," Jacob said. "But I want to talk to you about something other than this investigation."

I set aside my frustration at this unwelcome turn in the murder investigation. "Oh! An interesting case has appeared on your desk?"

"No, it's got nothing to do with work," Jacob said. "Well, in a roundabout way, it has, because that's where I was when I noticed this curious event."

"What would that be?" I asked.

"I believe we're being watched."

I glanced around. "By whom?"

"Not here and not now. But when I left the Margate office today, there was a distinctive dark car parked nearby."

"Who owned the car?" I asked. "Not a former client or someone you've put behind bars, was it? Someone unhappy and wanting revenge?"

"No. Nothing like that. This car came with a driver, and I'd recognise it anywhere. It belongs to Lady M."

My eyebrows sprang up. "Are you quite sure? What is she doing in Margate?"

"I wondered that myself. So I detoured around the block and approached the car from behind. The back window was slightly down, so it was easy to see Lady M in the back seat."

My heartbeat quickened. "Was Ruby with her?"

"No, at least she wasn't in the car when I passed," Jacob said.

"Why is Lady M following you?" I asked.

"I suspect I'm not the target. She's interested in you," Jacob said. "Ruby must be worried because you haven't replied to her letter. Perhaps Lady M undertook an adventure to find you."

I huffed out my disapproval. "Anyone would think I'm the one who's been hiding."

"Have you decided about writing back to Ruby?"

I toyed with my glass of gin fizz. "I don't know what to say. Part of me wants to accuse Ruby of lying and concealing matters of utmost importance. But I also want to forgive her. I have listened to you, and

I understand she may be hesitant to get me involved because I can sometimes be, well, occasionally bossy."

"Really? I hadn't noticed."

It was a wonder how Jacob prevented himself from smiling. "Don't tease me about something so important. If our friendship is so unbalanced, do we have a bond at all? I adore Ruby, and I always thought she knew I'd be there for her."

"This is an unusual situation," Jacob said. "Perhaps she needed time to puzzle things through. Now she knows the way forward, and she wants to get you involved in her plan."

"Ruby and plans rarely go together," I said.

"They'll need to now. It's not just herself she's thinking about," Jacob said. "A child changes everything."

I wrinkled my nose. "Ruby will no longer be footloose and fancy-free to come on our adventures." This was the start of tremendous change for both of us. It was a change I wasn't sure I could see through. But if I abandoned Ruby, was that the end of our friendship?

I finished my drink and set down the empty glass. "I need a long walk to get my thoughts in order."

"You can only go on so many walks before you make a decision," Jacob replied. "Let me come with you. We can talk things through."

"You're an angel, but only I can muddle through the inner workings of my mind. I need to get everything in order. And before you protest and mention my tendency for bossiness, that doesn't mean I plan to take over Ruby's life. I'll have to make adjustments, too. If I no longer have Ruby by my side in the same capacity, then things must change."

"Change can sometimes be for the better," Jacob said.

"It can also be a wretched nuisance. Stay here and finish your drink. I'll take a walk and then return to my lodgings. We can pick this up tomorrow over breakfast. I could come to Margate for the day, and we can sort through files together and find a juicy case to get lost in."

"I'd like that," Jacob said. "And by the end of tomorrow, we'll have more information from Bishop as to the progress made questioning Charles."

"They'll make no progress, and I'll have to resist saying I told him so." I kissed Jacob's cheek. "I'll see you in the morning."

I waved goodbye to Colin, who stood behind the bar, busy serving customers now the pub had reopened. I left the Green Man, planning a brisk walk along the quiet streets and out towards the marshes before it got dark.

Before I ventured far, I spotted a familiar figure. Samuel Drake lurked in the shadows, sliding past houses, eager not to draw attention to himself. When a man behaved like that, it made me keen to discover what shady business he was up to.

Benji was instantly on the alert, sensing me tense as I watched Samuel. He walked in the opposite direction to his antique shop, moving away from the houses. He was heading to the marsh, too.

"What's this sneaky chap up to?" I whispered to Benji.

Benji looked up at me, his ears pricked.

"Since he's going our way, it's not as if we're following him. Make sure you don't lose him, though."

Samuel's pace quickened as he left the populated areas and walked along a well-trodden path running beside the tidal creek. A hint of dusk surrounded us, and several bats flew over my head, enticed by water-loving insects.

The bats entranced Benji as we hurried along, but I kept Samuel in sight. I hoped he wouldn't double back, and this was a circular route that would lead him into town.

A much larger winged creature flitted close by, and a lone hoot revealed it to be an owl hunting for its evening meal. I watched the magnificent bird sweep around slowly, taking its time, but I still monitored Samuel.

Perhaps he was just out for an evening constitutional. It was a pleasant evening, although there was a nip in the air.

I walked along, flipping up my jacket collar to keep warm and swinging my arms. Benji was delighted to be romping free. Although he realised we were on a mission, he enjoyed taking his time to sniff the scents and explore the surroundings.

Then Samuel dropped out of sight. Gone! Just like that.

I stopped for a moment. Were my eyes playing tricks on me? Or had the man fallen into a hole? I broke into a run to locate the place where I'd last seen him. As I rounded a slight bend in the pathway, it became clear.

Hidden from plain sight was a small tunnel entrance. This must be an old smuggling route that started at the creek bank. I didn't think this one connected to the Green Man, because it would have to make some odd angles and diversions to get back to the pub. But I'd heard enough about the smuggling routes to know there were many tunnels leading from the creek into different buildings in the town.

"Let's see what Samuel is up to," I whispered to Benji. "I knew he couldn't be trusted." I slid down the steep bank to the tunnel entrance. It would have been easy to miss, since it was concealed by branches.

After examining the outside of the tunnel, I was satisfied it was safe. Someone had worked on it recently, adding ceiling beams and wooden struts to ensure the risk of collapse was minimal.

I snuck into the inky darkness, not a sniff of light to be had. The sky behind us was swiftly darkening, and for a moment, I wished I'd brought a torch. Benji crept along beside me, ever alert for risks. I stopped and cocked my head. There was a scuffling noise in front of us.

It sounded like digging. Not urgent, frantic pounding, but more like the careful scrape of an archaeologist's trowel as they uncovered some treasure long hidden in the dirt.

Benji growled softly, and I rested a hand on his head to reassure him.

The scraping sounds grew louder as we continued along the tunnel.

Was Samuel excavating? Perhaps he believed Edmund was onto something and close to finding the family fortune. That would only strengthen the motive against Samuel. If Edmund revealed he knew the location of the gold and gemstones, Samuel could have decided he no longer needed Edmund. Why not get rid of the competition and keep the fortune for himself?

I froze as the noises stopped, but a few seconds later, they began again. Benji growled another warning and then let out a most alarming bark, whirling around and lunging.

His warning that we weren't alone came a second too late, and I was only just turning when something hard slammed into the back of my neck.

# Chapter 19

A raspy, damp cloth rubbed against the end of my nose. I shifted my head to dislodge the unpleasant sensation, but it followed me, and I instantly regretted moving, as a troublesome thump rocketed through my skull.

As my senses returned to order, I grew aware I was on my side on cold stone. And the raspy cloth wasn't a cloth, but Benji's tongue, repeatedly licking across my face as I stirred back to consciousness.

He whimpered as my eyes inched open. I peered groggily at him, not yet certain the power of speech had returned.

Every muscle tightened as the realisation of how vulnerable I was slammed into me almost as hard as the object that had struck the back of my neck. I had to ensure we were out of danger.

I shifted, but even that fairy-like movement caused a fluttering wave of unconsciousness to nudge at me, showering my vision with black dots.

I took several tentative breaths, longing for the pain to dislodge from my head. Why was it always my head that was targeted? Although this blow had been at the base of my neck. If it had been much harder, something critical would have snapped, and I wouldn't be able to twitch my toes or wriggle my fingers.

Rather than moving, I risked an examination of the spot where I lay, only flicking my eyes about. I was in the tunnel.

I'd been so preoccupied by the scraping noises that I'd been too slow to realise danger was behind us. Despite Benji being quick, he hadn't been fast enough to stop our stealthy attacker. And they must have been furtive and silent to outwit Benji.

I shuffled a hand over to him and rested it on his head. If we were still in danger, Benji would sort them out. He was my stalwart protector, facing off against guns, foul men with dreadful tempers, and all manner of ne'er-do-wells. I felt safe under his watchful gaze.

After remaining on my side for ten minutes, several of which were spent with me slipping back into unconsciousness, I had to move. I was frozen through, and my teeth chattered.

With care, I inched myself up then rested against the wall, simply breathing until the nausea faded.

"What a pickle we've found ourselves in," I said to Benji, barely speaking above a whisper, because every word sent a shiver of pain down my spine.

A check of the time had me grimacing. It was past midnight. I should have been back at my lodgings hours ago. Jenny would be worried sick and would have contacted Jacob, so he'd be beside himself. He had no idea which direction I'd walked when we left him at the Green Man, so he wouldn't know where to look for me.

Benji leaned heavily against my leg, panting slightly, showing how stressed he was.

"Don't you worry about me. I've been through worse than this." Although it had been some time since I'd felt so dreadfully battered. My last brush with death had been during the Great War after I'd spent several days trapped in a tiny room, under threat of discovery by the enemy, who wanted to put a bullet between my eyes.

No, this wouldn't do. I wouldn't give in to my injury. My head throbbed every time I moved, but I could stand. And if that failed, I'd crawl to town on my hands and knees.

I looked along the dark tunnel. If I knew where the tunnel came out, I'd consider following it. But what if I got to the end and found the entrance locked? We'd have to retrace our steps and then walk across the marsh. I wasn't up to such a task.

Slowly and cautiously, I shuffled towards the tunnel exit. The night was pitch black. No hint of light from Faversham to aid our way, and the new moon was of little use.

Once I'd struggled up the bank and onto the path, I leaned forward and softly moaned.

Benji nudged me with his nose. I hadn't taken a step in at least a minute, so unsure was I on my feet.

"You're quite right. No dithering. You'll be cold, too. And hungry. We've missed your supper."

He whimpered softly and nudged me again. I hunted in my jacket pockets and found a few of his favourite treats, which I fed him, taking another moment to compose myself, and then I made a few tentative steps forward.

Although the progress was slow and my knees wobbly, I gained confidence as we edged closer to Faversham.

I stumbled on uneven ground, losing my balance and landing hard on my hands and knees. I may have grunted and moaned simultaneously since it was so jarring to my injuries. Benji was instantly by my side, nudging his head underneath my arm and licking my nose again.

"What a fool I am, not watching where I'm going," I muttered.

I eased myself back until I sat on my heels. There was something different about Benji's right paw. I gestured for him to lift it, which he did. There, caught between his nails, was a piece of torn cloth.

"You good boy. You attacked whoever did this to me, didn't you? And you collected evidence." I gently eased the cloth from beneath his claws. Although it was muddy and damp, I could tell it was velvet. There was a faint smell of flowers about it and a spot of what could be blood. A woman had attacked me!

There were female suspects in this investigation. I'd considered both May Shaw and Miss Florence Hatley. Was one of them working with Samuel? Had they arranged a meeting in the tunnel, and I'd disturbed things? Whoever saw me creeping after Samuel had tried to put me out of the picture, and they'd almost succeeded.

May was capable. And although Jacob and Bishop considered Miss Hatley a frail old lady, she was sprightlier than people realised.

I thought about the clothing they'd worn when I'd met them. They were practical dressers, much like me, but even I had a velvet jacket in my wardrobe, so this cloth might have come from either lady.

I tucked the fabric into a pocket and, after taking a few deep breaths of the bracing, chilly air, crept along the creek bank, with Benji carefully guiding me all the way.

It took several more stops and a few more stumbles, but I was glad to see lights as I continued to my lodgings.

Just as I reached the front door, it sprang open. Jacob was there, and standing right beside him, Jenny looked pale and anxious. Jacob rushed out and engulfed me in a welcome hug.

"Careful," I said. "I've had a blow to the head. Well, the neck. It's terribly sore."

He stepped back, keeping hold of my shoulders and dipping to look into my face. "Another blow to the head?"

"Neck. And this time from behind. I'd appreciate being able to sit. I'm not sure I can stand for much longer." It was rare that I admitted my weaknesses, so I must have been feeling it.

Jacob guided me into the kitchen, which was welcomingly warm and brightly lit. So bright it made me wince.

"Lord above, what have you got yourself into this time?" Jenny bustled close behind Jacob. She hurried over and crouched beside me. "You're covered in dirt, and you're paler than the ghost who haunts the old abbey."

"I'd appreciate a strong cup of tea, and something warm to apply to the back of my neck," I said.

"I'll deal with that," Jenny replied briskly. "Mr Templeton, there are blankets in the cupboard at the top of the stairs. Fetch them. She needs warming."

Jacob dashed away but was back within the minute and soon wrapping me in a clean, warm blanket, which I gratefully tucked around myself.

"I knew something was wrong when you didn't come back for a cup of tea before bed," Jenny said, as she poured boiling water into a large brown teapot. "I told myself not to worry, but since you had that blow to the head, I couldn't stop thinking about what trouble would find you now the O'Rourke family knows about you."

"Oh, I hadn't considered them," I replied. "Surely not. We've got the main troublemakers from that gang locked away."

"They're the most likely culprits of this assault," Jacob said. "And they're not beyond hitting a woman when she gets in their way. Tell us what happened."

As the tea brewed, I recounted my eventful evening. The walk with Benji, seeing Samuel and following him into a smuggler's tunnel.

I finished with, "Just before I was struck, Benji warned me we were in trouble, but I was too slow to respond. I got a thump on the back of the neck and woke still inside the tunnel."

"Did you say the entrance was down a steep bank?" Jenny asked, freshening our tea.

"Yes. Partly hidden by carefully placed bushes and branches," I said.

"That tunnel leads from the creek to the butcher's shop. It's on the same street as the Green Man, just at the end of the row," Jenny said. "It's fortunate you didn't go along there. No one would have heard you. You'd have been stuck and unable to get out until the morning."

"And with that injury, you might not have survived the night," Jacob said. "I insist you see the doctor."

I considered protesting but decided against it. I felt dreadful.

"You'll have to wake him," Jenny said. "He's over on Tanners Street. Number seven. He's used to people knocking at his door at all hours."

Jacob left me in Jenny's capable care, and she tucked another blanket around me and cut me a thick slice of sponge cake. It had a delicious-looking layer of cream and jam in the middle, but I had no appetite.

"Would you mind feeding Benji?" I asked her. "He'll be starving after our adventures."

"I've got leftover steak and kidney pudding, if that will do." Jenny set out a generous portion of cold pudding for Benji on the floor, and after he looked at it, then looked at me for a second, he tucked in with vigour.

"He's such a good boy," I said. "He woke me by licking my face."

"There's nothing so loyal as a dog," Jenny said, as she settled back into her seat. "Are you sure it was a lady who hit you with such force?"

"Some gentlemen wear velvet, but not doused in something so fragrant," I said. "If I can find the item of clothing Benji tore, I'll learn who attacked me."

"There are plenty of finely dressed ladies in town, but I can't imagine any of them being so cruel." Jenny shuddered. "It does my heart no good to think there's someone so cold-blooded living nearby."

"We're close to catching them," I said. "They must be worried if they're going around thumping me on the head in the hopes of silencing me."

"You're lucky they didn't check to make sure they'd done a good job," Jenny said. "You were defenceless."

"I'm never defenceless with Benji by my side," I said. "You should get a dog. A lady living on her own needs a loyal watchdog. We rescued several dogs from the O'Rourke family. They'll need good homes after their rehabilitation."

"I'll consider that," Jenny said. "Perhaps you could introduce us. I want nothing big or noisy. But something loyal, just like your Benji."

"We'll make the arrangements," I said.

"She's in here." Jacob's voice carried along the hallway before he entered the kitchen, closely followed by a man in his forties, his round glasses sitting slightly askew on a long nose.

"Doctor Foster. Cup of tea?" Jenny asked.

"Thank you. That would be most agreeable." The doctor had a long face, much like his nose, and a kindly expression as he took a few minutes examining me while running through a series of questions to assess my ailments.

I answered with tired acceptance, although all I wanted to do was to retire to bed and forget this evening had ever happened.

"You'll feel sore for a week or two," Doctor Foster said after finishing his examination. "I'm recommending you go to the local cottage hospital. With a recent blow to the front of your head, and now this injury to your neck, we can't be too careful."

"It's not that bad, is it?" I asked.

"Listen to the doctor," Jacob said.

"It will only be for overnight observation," Doctor Foster added. "You've had a lucky escape. A blow in such a spot can sever nerves and connective tissue, leaving one paralysed."

"Does that mean whoever hit me wasn't particularly strong? Or they didn't want to kill me?" I asked.

Doctor Foster startled slightly. "I couldn't say. But it was a hard enough blow to mean business. Careful observation and an X-ray are needed. I'll make the arrangements."

I pressed my lips together then grimly nodded.

"I'll go with you," Jacob said.

"There's no need," I replied. "All I'll do is sleep or get prodded by nurses."

"I want to get you checked in and ensure you have everything you need," Jacob insisted.

Doctor Foster stood and tucked away his equipment. "I'll get things moving if I may use your telephone, Jenny."

"You know where it is," she said. "Come back here and have another cup of tea once you're done. I have rock cakes. I know how much you like them."

"Indeed, I do! Thank you." Doctor Foster hurried away.

"I must speak to May Shaw," I said. "She was the first person who came to mind when I woke. She wants to preserve the past, not plunder it. Perhaps she was sneaking in to confront Samuel and stop him from stealing. She saw me and thought I was about to plunder the treasure, so attacked. How about we—"

"That's quite enough of that," Jacob said firmly. "No more hard thoughts. You're injured, and my nerves are frazzled. You must rest."

"I agree with your gentleman friend," Jenny said. "I know you want to solve Edmund's murder, but if you end up the same way he did, it'll do no one any good."

"It'll definitely do my heart no good," Jacob said. "Nor Benji's. He keeps whimpering."

I looked at my sad-eyed dog and gave him a reassuring pat. "Well, I don't want Benji to feel bad. Very well. I'll try not to think about the murder. But first thing in the morning, we're solving this crime. I'm done with getting whacked on the head in the name of justice. It's time to solve this mystery once and for all."

# Chapter 20

Rolling onto a sore spot shook me from my most delicious slumber. For a few seconds, I couldn't place where I was. Then the events of last night tumbled into place. Jacob and Doctor Foster had insisted I stay in the cottage hospital overnight for observation. Although I was barely observed, or at least I don't recall being.

I'd received marvellous pain relief and had been unable to keep my eyes open. They'd stayed shut for goodness knows how long, since I no longer had my watch to check the time. But a warm sun shone through a gap in the curtain, so I knew I'd had a decent amount of sleep.

Not that it made my bumps and bruises feel any friendlier. If anything, they were worse. It was often the way with such injuries. The tenderness went on for days as the bruises changed colour.

I was inching up in bed, attempting to find a comfortable way to sit, when there was a smart tap on the closed door to my private room. A second later, an efficient-looking nurse breezed in.

"At last, you're awake. I was thinking there might be something seriously wrong with you, since you wouldn't stir. I was about to summon the doctor."

"Good morning to you, too," I said. "How long have I been asleep?"

"Twelve hours." The nurse pulled back the curtains, allowing sunlight to stream through and dazzle me.

"Goodness, that's far too long. I have so much to do." I attempted to slide out of bed, but the nurse hurried over and stopped me.

"You rest. The doctor needs to see you before you're discharged. Besides, you have a visitor."

"I'm hardly in any state for visitors," I said. "Unless it's my dog, Benji."

"No animals allowed. It's your gentleman friend! The tall, dark, and handsome one with the limp. I'll send him in with your breakfast, since you missed the early round."

My stomach grumbled an agreement, and I attempted to smooth my hair, although I don't know why I bothered. Jacob had seen me in dishevelled creations of my own making on more than one occasion, so I had little care what he thought of my physical appearance. Well, almost.

The nurse left, and a moment later, Jacob pushed through the door, coming in backwards and carrying a laden tray of breakfast items.

"Whyever did you let me sleep so late?" I admonished him. "We have a murder to solve!"

He smiled as he set the tray down so it rested on my knees. "I stopped by first thing, and the nurse said you weren't to be disturbed. You'd had a good night, but you needed rest, so I was to come back in a couple of hours."

"You shouldn't have listened to her. You know how busy we are." I gave in to my hunger and attacked the toast and marmalade while Jacob poured the tea.

"I know you're determined to solve this mystery," he said, "but you can't do that with a head injury."

"I've been managing perfectly well with the first injury," I said.

"Is that so? Or were you off your game when you went into that tunnel?" Jacob settled on the edge of the bed. "Perhaps that first bump on the head meant you missed a few clues."

I scowled at him. "I never miss clues."

"You missed someone sneaking up behind you."

I crunched on my toast noisily, angry he pointed out an obvious truth I didn't want to accept.

"Have you remembered anything new from last night?" Jacob asked. "Anything come to mind to give you a clue who hit you?"

"Only the piece of cloth Benji grabbed from my attacker," I said. "How is he? Is he with Jenny?"

"She kept him overnight, but I dropped Benji off at the Green Man this morning," Jacob said. "He was happy to stay, since Colin had a huge plate of bacon and eggs, and I'm sure Benji would get some."

"My dog loves his breakfast food," I said with a small smile. "After this, I'll dress and we'll return to the smugglers' tunnel. In the daylight, we may see something useful."

"The doctor said you can leave?" Jacob asked.

"That nurse is making arrangements," I replied. "I feel fine. And I'm missing Benji dreadfully."

Jacob shook his head. "It's too risky to go back. They're on to you."

"Who are you referring to?" I asked.

"I thought we decided it was the O'Rourke family who did this to you." Jacob took a piece of my buttered toast and took a bite.

"I didn't see anyone, so I can't confirm that," I said. "The only thing I know is the hidden treasure is worth killing for."

"Exactly my point. I don't want you to be the next victim."

I set down my toast crust and took a long drink of tea. "We're close to figuring it out. This injury won't defeat me."

"Maybe there's nothing left to fight for," Jacob said. "Bishop is holding Charles."

"Has he confessed to murdering Edmund?"

"Charles's alibi is unreliable," Jacob said.

"I'll admit, the word of a hardened criminal isn't the best word to rely upon, but Mickey gains nothing from Charles going to prison."

"It's more complicated than that. Bishop found Charles after he broke into Edmund's house. He was ransacking the place. Stockpiling things he thought had value."

"Did he break in, or does he have a key?" I asked. "Since Charles will inherit Edmund's estate, are his actions even criminal?"

"He was loading things into sacks and going through all the drawers."

"Charles could just be an efficient chap, wanting to deal with his brother's affairs swiftly," I said.

"Charles was jealous of Edmund. Edmund had a stable life, a good career, and a home of his own. Charles was on the streets and had a gambling problem. He needed money fast."

I remained unconvinced. "What about this mysterious female accomplice?"

"She may not even exist!"

"I've been thinking. What if May wasn't there to confront Samuel, but they're working together? She's dangerous," I said. "Samuel's partner in crime was prepared to do me serious harm because I stood in the way."

"Yes. Quite literally," Jacob said. "You must take a step back. You can't afford any more injuries."

"I refuse to. I'm not happy the police believe Charles committed this murder."

"For now, find a way to make yourself happy," Jacob said. "You're on bed rest and recovery until further notice."

"Nonsense. Unless Charles makes a full confession, I won't be able to settle," I said. "What if the police charge the wrong man, and a killer walks away? They could use their freedom to uncover the Blackwood family fortune and believe murder pays off. They could do it again."

"There is no family fortune," Jacob said. "Maybe there are a few old bits and pieces buried under the mud, but it won't make anyone rich."

"We should still keep investigating," I insisted. "We don't want to miss anything."

"All you need to focus on is eating toast, drinking your tea, and then I'm taking you home to rest. That's assuming the doctor says you can leave today."

I grumbled to myself and ate three more slices of toast. Despite what the police thought, this matter felt unresolved. There were viable suspects in Edmund's murder, and I couldn't believe a man as discombobulated as Charles could formulate a plan to murder his only family. That needed cunning. Someone who could sneak into the pub without drawing attention, commit the dreadful deed, and leave again. Charles was a clumsy, nervous wreck. The task was beyond him.

It had to be someone smart. And sly. Someone who had lied to me. I still thought that someone was Samuel.

Two hours later, and after being prodded and poked about and having the doctor circle me like I was an exhibition in an artist's studio, I was allowed to leave the hospital.

I was desperate to stretch my legs and walk off the feeling of being an invalid. I despised sickness. It was a most unproductive state to be in.

Jacob had his car, so we travelled back to Faversham in a comfortable silence. He stopped outside the Green Man pub, since I was eager to see Benji.

I'd just stepped out of the car when I spotted William and his pretty fiancée, Elizabeth, walking towards us, their heads bent close together in an intense conversation.

"Will you look at that?" I said to Jacob.

"What am I supposed to be observing?"

"How pale William's fiancée is. That's what wedding planning does to a person."

He chuckled. "I didn't realise William was engaged to be married."

"I heard from a reliable source that he planned to ask Elizabeth to be his wife. He must have done so because the poor dear looks half frightened to death."

"If I ever convince you to marry me," Jacob said lightly, "I'll plan everything. That way, you won't have to worry about growing pale and anxious."

I glanced at him and gave a loud, haughty snort. "Provided Benji is there, we can marry in a shed for all I care."

"Well now, that's a turn-up for the books," Jacob said, grinning. "That was almost a yes."

"Indeed, it was. I must have been hit harder than I realised." I gave his arm a good-natured squeeze. "Let's go fix this muddle, shall we?"

---

Jacob had remained by my side for most of the day until I'd chased him away in the evening after we'd dined together. I enjoyed his company, but I needed space, and Benji and I were overdue a stroll around town.

I gave it ten minutes after Jacob left, in case he lurked about to see if I misbehaved. Then, I put on my most comfortable walking shoes and headed out the front door with Benji, calling out to Jenny to let her know I wouldn't be long.

I took a deep, welcome breath as I marched along, happy to be outside. All this confinement made one feel like a Victorian waif, too weak to rise from a comfortable armchair and deal with life in all its messy glory.

This was the ticket. Fresh air, exercise, and time and space to think through the Edmund situation. The solution was in front of me. I'd met all the suspects, determined their motives, checked alibis, but I was still missing something.

A confession would be handy. Why did the guilty not simply admit to their bad deeds? Some people's moral compasses were seriously skewed.

"Shall we visit Bishop and see if he's at his desk?" I said to Benji. "After all, he promised to keep us informed."

Benji was always happy to go wherever I took him. As I turned onto the main street in search of the local police station, he trotted beside me, tail wagging and nose snuffling.

I entered the small, tidy lobby of the station and found a friendly-faced female officer on duty. I announced myself and asked to speak to Detective Bishop.

"You're in luck, miss," she said. "He's just come off shift. He's sorting his paperwork. I'll give him a shout."

I thanked her and walked around, glancing at the neatly pinned notices and posters about various community activities in Faversham.

A few minutes later, Bishop appeared.

"I'm glad to see you back on your feet," he said. "Jacob told me what's been going on. I've been worried about you."

"Yes, my head has been a particular target during this investigation," I said.

"Back and front! You need to be careful."

"I spent a restorative night in the hospital. I'm fully restored," I said. "But I need your assistance."

"I suppose you want an update on the case?"

"Not quite. Although I'd appreciate that too," I said.

"Come through. This calls for a cup of tea and a sit-down."

Five minutes later, I nursed a stewed cup of tea and decided Bishop was a practical man, so he'd appreciate a sensible approach.

"What can I do for you?" he asked.

"I need to speak to Mickey O'Rourke."

His hand froze mid-reach for a pencil. "Why do you want to speak to that lowlife?"

"I could deceive you and say I wanted to give him a piece of my mind about the illegal dog fights," I said. "But I have my concerns about Charles's guilt. From what Jacob told me, you don't consider Mickey's alibi reliable. And before you protest, I understand why. But I don't think Charles murdered Edmund."

"I figured you wanted to scold him. Jacob believes it was one of the O'Rourke gang members who whacked you in the smuggling tunnel."

"I'm not so sure about that either."

He tilted his head, curious. "You have another theory?"

"Did Jacob mention that Benji grabbed my attacker and tore off a piece of their clothing?" I asked. "It was velvet and had a floral scent. Do you think a member of the O'Rourke family would swan around in velvet, smelling like a lady?"

Bishop blinked. "Unlikely. Jacob said something about a piece of cloth, yes."

"I have it right here." I fished into my coat pocket and pulled it out, placing the grubby scrap on his desk. "A lady would wear that, not a gentleman. And if you sniff it, you'll see what I mean about the scent. Although it's faded."

He brought it delicately to his nose and gave it a cautious sniff. "There is something floral. But maybe it picked that up from the ground?"

"There are no flowers near the smuggling tunnel. It's a clue. And if we want to get to the bottom of what really happened to Edmund, we must follow every lead, no matter how small."

Bishop looked at me with the weariness of a man who knew he was about to be talked into something against his better judgement.

"I know you told me to tread carefully in this investigation," I continued. "But we have to make sure we get the right person. You understand my character. I'm not likely to make rash decisions or do anything foolish."

Bishop's gaze flicked to the injury on my head.

I touched the healing bump and smiled wryly. "You understand my meaning. Not intentionally foolish. Perhaps I take a risk or two, but I always get the job done."

"And you believe speaking to Mickey will get the job done?"

I leaned in. "All I'm asking for is ten minutes with Mickey O'Rourke. I want to find out if he lied about what Charles did on the night of the murder."

He sighed. "I appreciate your thoroughness, but we've done everything by the book. Charles had every reason to want his brother dead."

"Please," I said softly. "You'd be helping me in my hour of need."

Bishop chuckled. "You don't strike me as a lady who's ever in serious need."

"Then call it a professional courtesy. Edmund died in my pub. I must know his killer is off the streets for good."

He sighed again and sat back in his chair, studying me. "Since I hear nothing but good things about you from Jacob, let me see what I can do. No promises. You sit here and drink your tea."

"You're an excellent fellow," I said as he stood to leave.

"Excellent or foolish when you're involved. I've yet to decide."

Hurray! We had progress. Now, all I had to do was convince an unscrupulous scoundrel to be honest for once, and the mystery would be solved.

# Chapter 21

The interview room was small, square, and smelled faintly of old cigarettes. A single table dominated the middle of the room, flanked by two hard chairs. I sat in one, hands folded neatly on the table. The opposite chair scraped across the floor as Mickey O'Rourke slumped into it, all surly attitude and suspicious eyes.

He didn't look at me right away. Instead, he glanced towards the open door, where Bishop lingered just out of sight but well within earshot. I felt reassured knowing he was there. Not that I expected Mickey to leap across the table and throttle me, but one could never be too careful when confronting criminals with bruised egos. Especially when I'd been the one to bruise them.

"Well," Mickey said at last, his voice like gravel dragged over concrete. "What's this about, then? You fancy playing detective, do you?"

"I never play," I replied.

His upper lip curled, and I caught the flicker of a smirk before it vanished behind a wall of irritation and hardness.

"Didn't think they let nosy women play at coppers," he muttered.

"These are modern times. Someone murdered Edmund Blackwood in my pub, and I'd like to know why."

Mickey leaned back in the chair, arms crossed, muscles flexing beneath a battered jacket. "Do you think I did it?"

"I think you might know who did."

Mickey scowled, eyes narrowing. "You know, your little mutt took a chunk out of my brother. He should be shot."

"That's no way to speak about your brother."

Mickey hissed at me.

"I feel the same about the many criminals I deal with," I said. "Although I reserve the death sentence for people who are cruel to animals."

He went quiet. A muscle ticked in his clenched jaw. "Some dogs like to fight. It's in their nature."

"A dog is only as well-mannered as his owner. But we aren't here to discuss that. Charles said he was running from you the night Edmund died. You confirmed that. Were you being truthful?"

"I don't owe you anything," he snapped.

"You owe Charles something, since you've been terrifying him."

"He owes me money!" Mickey slammed his fist on the table. I didn't flinch. Behind him, I saw Bishop shift slightly in the doorway, his attention sharpening.

"A tantrum will simply see you put back in your cell," I said.

"You don't know what you're talking about," Mickey growled.

"Then enlighten me."

He stood suddenly, paced to the wall and back and ran a hand through his cropped hair. Then he turned and jabbed a finger towards me. "You don't know what this life is like. With your posh voice and clothes. You don't know hardness."

"You're avoiding the question," I said. "Was Charles fleeing from you on the night of Edmund's murder?"

He stared at me, breathing hard.

"Your intimidation tactics don't work on me. All I care about is getting to the truth. You can help with that, or you can carry on snarling and stomping about like an ill-tempered bull."

Mickey stared at me for a long moment then let out a low grunt. "You're not what I expected."

"You're exactly what I expected. How disappointing," I said.

He laughed without humour. "You've got no idea what you're sticking your nose into. I'm sharing nothing with you. Why should I, when you lost me my income?"

"Anyone who earns money in such a disgusting fashion deserves to have it taken," I said. "You must know those dogs were terrified. They didn't want to fight each other. I can guarantee the little ones didn't want to be bait. What you did was a terrible thing."

"How else am I supposed to earn money?"

"Through good, honest, hard work."

Mickey sneered at me. "I wouldn't do it if the men didn't come and pay their coin."

"You should be ashamed of yourself. So should they."

He glowered at me from under thick eyebrows. "It's a family business. We've always done it. It's tradition."

"Just because something is a tradition doesn't mean it's right," I said. "Times are changing, and you need to move with them, or you find yourself in this position."

"Because of you! You're the reason I'm here. You stuck your nose into things that don't concern you."

"Is that why you sent somebody after me?" I asked.

A flash of confusion crossed Mickey's face. "Sent someone? You've got it wrong. How would I do that from inside a cell?"

"Perhaps you instructed a visitor to teach me a lesson."

"They haven't allowed me any." He shot a filthy look at the open door.

"What about a telephone call?"

"Who would I call? No one wants to help me. And my brothers are already locked up. No thanks to you."

I glanced at the door, and Bishop gave me a nod to show Mickey told the truth about having no contact with the outside world.

"You must have been upsetting somebody else," Mickey said. "It's no surprise they walloped you. I would again, given half a chance."

"What impeccable manners you have," I said.

"You don't learn manners when you have to fight to survive."

I noticed a flicker of exhaustion in Mickey's shoulders. "Life can be cruel, but that doesn't mean you have to be."

He heaved out a breath and returned to his chair. "My old pops set up the dog ring. He got men paying to see the fights. Then we caught those who found themselves in bother when paying back the money we loaned them, and the business grew."

"And you were happy to pocket the profit, not caring about the misery you caused."

"Show me an employer who'd take on an old crook who can't even read."

"That can be remedied if you're willing to learn."

Mickey snorted derisively. "At my age? I could never get those letters to make sense. When I stared at a page, they floated. I couldn't understand what people talked about when they read. So, I made excuses then stopped going to class. It was easier than being made to look the fool. And I'm not. I've proved that by keeping the fight rings going and turning a profit."

"Did you ever see a doctor about your floating words?" I asked.

"He wouldn't know what to do with me. I made my way in this world, and I'm a success."

"But are you a happy success?" I asked. "Did seeing those poor dogs destroyed bring you peace?"

"I've no need for peace. Just as long as I have money in my pocket and a safe place to stay, that's the main thing." Mickey slid a glance at me. "Besides, some of them made it."

I sat up straight. "What do you mean?"

"A few of the dogs worked the rings successfully, but they got too old to keep fighting. My pops would get rid of them. Well, he'd tell one of his men to do it. When he died and I took over, I decided not to."

My breath caught. "If you didn't get rid of them, what did you do with them?"

Mickey wouldn't meet my gaze. "You'll think I'm soft if I tell you."

"Soft? That suggests you did them no harm." A flicker of hope lit inside me. Perhaps Mickey O'Rourke wasn't bad through and through.

"I found an abandoned bit of land with a couple of sheds no one was using. I stuck fencing up, tidied the sheds, and retired the dogs there. It's not a life of luxury, but it's warm and dry. I go over daily, feed them, and let them have a wander."

Unexpected tears sprang to my eyes. "That's wonderful. After so much trauma, the dogs need a safe space."

Mickey shuffled in his seat and shrugged his shoulders up and down several times. "Maybe I don't love the fight rings, but it's all I know. I can't change things now. My brothers wouldn't stand for it. They'd kick me out. Laugh at me. It would be like being back at school. I hated that place."

"Mickey, you're in serious trouble because of the dogfights and the stealing," I said. "If you focus on a legal business, your brothers would be happier. They wouldn't constantly look over their shoulders in fear of being arrested again."

"They're too set in their ways to change. So am I. Once they get out, they'll go right back to their old ways. So will I."

"I don't believe that. And you've proven you can change by setting up a retirement home for older dogs. No matter your past, you can make a positive difference."

"It was nothing. I just didn't want to... you know. Finish them off myself."

"It was everything to those dogs. Yes, you mistreated them by forcing them to fight to earn money for you, but you gave them a good end. A kinder end than your father would have done."

Mickey grimaced. "He was a hard man. Never had time for anyone unless he could make money off them. Including me. As soon as I said I was struggling at school, he yanked me out and sent me to work."

"I'm sorry to hear that," I said. "He should have taken better care of you."

"It's in the past, and you can't change that."

I sat back in my seat and studied Mickey for several seconds until he glared at me.

"What are you looking at?" he grumbled.

"I have an idea," I said. "You won't be aware, but we've recently arranged with Lord Faversham to set up a dogs' home."

His expression brightened. "Like my shelter?"

"Exactly that. But on a bigger scale. And we'll need plenty of help."

"It takes time to look after them dogs," Mickey said. "Someone with Lord Faversham's clout will stuff money in your pockets to ensure they're happy. I always see him striding about with those well-fed dogs of his. He treats them like children."

"Yes, he's an advocate for the animals," I said. "And it appears you are, too."

"You've lost me."

"If you reform, you could be a part of something positive and stop the cruelty."

"Reform? You mean serve my time?"

"You may have a sentence to serve," I said, "but I'm friendly with an officer here. I could put in a good word for you."

"Why do that? You know what I was doing with those dogs. You told me yourself I was a bad person."

"You've surprised me, and few people do that," I said. "Yes, you may believe the only way you can earn money is by using those dogs, but then you showed them kindness. You showed you have goodness. And I think it wants to come out more."

Mickey coughed roughly and patted his chest. "Most people say they're just animals and they don't feel or understand, so it doesn't matter what we do to them."

"But you have your doubts?" I asked.

"You'll think this is daft, but I see them having different manners and ways about them. Like people, I suppose."

"That makes perfect sense to me," I said. "I've spent my life around rescue animals, and as you know, I have a dog of my own. We rescued each other many years ago."

Mickey grunted. "For a small thing, he was feistier than I expected."

"Benji is loyal, stalwart, and any misdeeds he encounters, he deals with."

Mickey huffed a laugh through his nose. "Much like you, I suppose."

"We are similar," I said. "And I believe, as you do, that animals are more complicated than people realise. They have personalities, likes, dislikes, and habits. You need that kind of understanding to be involved at the dogs' home. What do you say?"

He shook his head, looking stunned. "You're giving me a second chance?"

"You know what you've done is wrong. That doesn't absolve you from your misdeeds, and you'll have to accept your punishment, but you deserve another try."

Mickey scrubbed the back of his hand across his eyes. "No one has ever offered to help me. My dad always said I was a useless sack of spuds and I'd end up dead in the gutter. Everyone would be glad when I died."

"It's time you prove him wrong," I said. "What do you say? Purposeful work. Helping animals in need. No more dog fights."

He sniffed back tears. "I say yes!"

"Excellent. Now, no more blubbering. I'll need trustee approval to bring you on board, but this could be the start of something. Rehabilitating dogs and assisting people who've fallen foul of the law."

Mickey gulped. "I... I don't know how to repay you."

"Be honest with me," I said. "I'm still investigating Edmund Blackwood's murder. The police have his brother Charles as the chief suspect. They believe his alibi is unreliable because you provided it."

He snorted his displeasure, and the hardness returned to his face. "That idiot Charlie-boy is innocent. I know the coppers don't think much of what I say, but I spoke the truth. I was hot on Charlie's heels that night, chasing him through the streets for two hours. He failed to show up to repay his debt, so me and the lads went looking for him. Faversham isn't that big, and we know his usual haunts. But he's quick on his feet, so he kept giving us the slip."

"Are you willing to give the names of the gentlemen who assisted you in tracking Charles down?" I asked.

"They'll hate talking to the coppers," Mickey said.

"Maybe so, but I'd appreciate your help," I said. "And the police will look favourably on you for assisting them in solving this murder. Maybe you will get to work with the dogs even sooner than you expected."

He grumbled under his breath for a few seconds before saying, "I'll give you their names."

I wrote the names he provided, intending to pass them out to Bishop.

"What will you do with that information?" he asked, eyeing me sharply as I folded the note and tucked it away.

"Simple. Solve this murder once and for all before anyone else gets bopped on the head."

# Chapter 22

"Jenny, you've outdone yourself with this continental breakfast." I was overwhelmed and thrilled when Jenny presented me with something different to the usual cooked breakfast.

She beamed at me. "I'm getting a younger crowd booking in, and not all of them want a greasy cooked breakfast, but toast and marmalade isn't enough to keep them full when they go off on day trips."

"I'm always partial to a sausage." Jacob sat opposite me, having joined me for breakfast in my lodgings, "but I'd be happy to eat this again. The cured meat is delicious."

"I'm not sure about the cold meat." Jenny peered at the plate.

"It goes nicely with the cheese," Jacob replied.

"When I was in France, this kind of breakfast was typical." I sipped from my cup of tea. "Although they served strong coffee with it."

"I'll try that," Jenny said. "Were you in France for a holiday?"

"Not quite," I said. "I skipped across the Channel during the war a time or two."

"Oh, like that, was it?" Jenny nodded, as if she knew exactly what I'd got up to during the Great War. "I spent most of my time turning my enormous garden into an allotment. I was always out and about with my vegetables, ensuring the elderly had something to eat."

"That was decent of you," I said.

Once Jenny assured herself we had everything we needed, she bustled off to do the laundry.

"I heard from Bishop first thing this morning," Jacob said.

"Has Charles confessed?" I asked. "Or was I right, and he's innocent?"

Jacob pressed his lips together. "He's refusing to say anything other than he's not guilty."

"As I thought. And after my conversation with Mickey, I'm even more convinced of that. Has Bishop spoken to Mickey's acquaintances to confirm Charles's innocence?"

"He's working on it. I'm not happy you went to see Mickey without me," Jacob said.

"Just because we're fond acquaintances doesn't mean you must follow me around like Benji," I said. "One loyal hound is quite enough."

"I know you're capable, but Mickey O'Rourke is dangerous."

"He was all bluster and glowers," I said. "Mickey is a scoundrel and has had an unpleasant life, but I saw a tiny spark of good in him."

Jacob grunted. He'd not been convinced when I'd told him about Mickey's sad past and his fondness for dogs, but I was determined to see if Mickey's good would shine through.

"I plan to visit Samuel after breakfast," I said. "He lied about his alibi, and I want to know about his female accomplice."

"Leave that to the police," Jacob said.

"They've done nothing! And they're only interested in Charles, despite me handing them evidence to show he's not guilty."

"You're too impatient."

"I am when a murder remains unsolved. You should be, too."

Jacob folded a piece of cured meat around a lump of cheese. "I could cancel my appointment this morning and come with you."

"As I've said, there's no need for you to accompany me everywhere. Besides, you have an important case meeting. You can't afford to miss it."

"It is an interesting case," Jacob said. "I'd like us to work on it."

"Then go to the meeting and make the arrangements," I said. "They'd be a fool not to hire us. Well, hire you. After this adventure, I must return to London and ensure my mother and Matthew have been behaving. Although I've had a delightful time in Kent."

"Getting whacked on the head is delightful?"

I gently swatted his hand. "I meant spending time with you."

"You should visit more often. Unless you find me too vexing," Jacob said.

"As if I ever would!"

He raised an eyebrow. "I'm aware of why you set up our private investigation service."

"There are always people who need such important services."

"True enough, but after my accident, there was no opportunity for me in the police," Jacob said. "I would have withered with boredom if you hadn't devised our private detective agency. Just far enough away so we don't trip over each other, yet close enough to offer support when needed."

I feigned innocence. "You had the right skills. It was the perfect opportunity, and we had the finances to ensure it could happen."

"And you wanted to give me a purpose," Jacob said.

I set down my cup. "Is that such a bad thing?"

"No. I'm grateful for it." Jacob took hold of my hand. "Just don't stay away for too long. Your life in London keeps you busy, but we have a life together, too. It may not be as conventional as most, but I want it to progress. We tease about marriage, but that's what I want for us."

I'd always declared I'd never marry. It seemed a pointless task. If you found a chap you liked, you rubbed along nicely until it was no longer pleasant, and then moved on. Why shackle yourself to such an outdated institution?

He shook his head and smiled good-naturedly, as if he could read my thoughts. "Perhaps one day I'll change your mind, but for now, that mind of yours is set on another course."

"That course most definitely involves you," I said. "I'm delighted to have you in my life, and I'm thrilled our agency is thriving."

"Then I'll be the one to change," Jacob said. "When it comes to you, I have a surprising amount of patience."

"It's perhaps for the best," I replied. "I can be a touch stubborn when making any significant shifts."

"I can't say I'd noticed."

I chuckled as I stood from the table. "Have a productive day. I'll give you an update on what Samuel tells me later."

"Watch your back when you talk to him," Jacob said. "And make sure no one sneaks up behind you this time."

"I can assure you, I won't make that mistake again." I kissed him lightly on the cheek, prepared myself to leave the lodgings, and then exited with Benji, leaving Jacob to finish the breakfast spread.

We made the short walk to the antique shop, and I was happy to see it open. I strode in, marching to the counter where Samuel stood.

He looked mildly surprised by my strident action, his features hardening as I drew near. "Please don't tell me I must deal with a second hysterical female this morning."

"A second? To whom are you referring?"

"It doesn't matter. No one needs such trouble so early in the day."

"I've never been hysterical in my life," I said. "I'll cut straight to the point. I know you lied about your alibi, and I intend to tell the police."

Samuel froze, mid-polish of a small silver salt and pepper shaker set. "Whatever do you mean?"

"I visited the Lobster Pot, where you take your clients. It was charming, and the view was spectacular. I had an illuminating conversation with the manager."

"Mr Lewis wouldn't tell you anything. He values his loyal customers, and he's discreet. It's the reason I go there."

"I'll admit, at first he was reticent, but when he learnt you're implicated in a murder, he decided he didn't want his restaurant connected to a dangerous criminal."

Samuel thumped the pepper shaker down and glowered at me. "I had nothing to do with Edmund's death. I've told the police that, and they believe me."

"They'll change their minds after I've spoken to them," I said.

"You'll do no such thing! The police have a man in custody for Edmund's murder. I was in the Green Man last night and heard all about it. You're wasting your time coming after me."

"Your accomplice knocked me senseless. I'm lucky to be alive."

His head jerked back. "My accomplice?"

"I followed you the other evening when you went into the smugglers' tunnel," I said. "I intended to see what you were up to, but I was caught unawares and whacked on the back of the head. Don't say you didn't see me unconscious when you left."

Samuel blinked rapidly, confusion crossing his face. "I didn't see you. But I wouldn't have done. Was it serious?"

"I had to spend the night in the local hospital," I replied.

"I'm sorry to hear that. How are you feeling?"

His concern surprised me. "I'm a fast healer. I have an excellent constitution. The same can't be said for your manners or morals, leaving an injured woman abandoned in the dark with a serious head injury."

"No, you misunderstand me," Samuel said quickly. "I didn't see you because I didn't walk back along the river. The tunnel leads to the butcher's shop. I have an arrangement with him, and he gave me a key to get in and out. He knows I go into the tunnels at night." He extracted a key from his pocket and held it up. "If I'd seen you injured, I would have helped you."

"Not if you thought I'd scupper your plans to steal the Blackwood treasure," I said.

"I'm stealing nothing!" Samuel replied. "No one has a claim on anything in those tunnels. After all, it's smuggled loot."

"You admit that's what you were looking for?" I asked.

He sighed and placed the key back in his pocket. "I am. Edmund claimed it was buried in a particular section of the tunnel. He even claimed to have a map and told me he was close to finding it. He pleaded for more financing to shore up and expand a section because it was at risk of collapse."

I kept the information that I had such map tucked away in a pocket to myself. "You didn't believe he was on to something?"

"I wasn't convinced there was a fortune to be found."

"So why continue the search on your own?"

Samuel didn't speak for several seconds, his gaze casting about the shop. "Edmund brought me a few bits. He claimed he'd dug them out of the tunnel. Coins, rings, a few old weapons. That sort of thing. It got me to thinking... what if he was right and I was passing up the opportunity of my life? I had to check."

"I'd appreciate seeing those finds," I said. "But bring them here. I'd prefer not to be alone with you, in case I get walloped on the head again."

Samuel frowned. "You're wasting your time. That wasn't me."

"It was your accomplice. I heard you digging in the tunnel. But we'll get to that in a moment."

"I don't have an accomplice." His bottom lip jutted out when he realised I was staying put until I got the information I needed. "Wait here. I'll bring out a few items." Samuel disappeared and returned a few moments later, carrying a large tray laden with various objects. There were gold coins, two rings set with precious stones, a tray of ivory-handled knives, and a small cloth-filled sack.

"Do you know what material those knife handles are made from?" I glowered at the items.

"Of course! I'm an expert in my field."

"And you have no concerns about the animals the ivory came from?"

Samuel lifted one shoulder. "I find what is in demand. There's no accounting for taste."

The procurement of ivory so people could have what they considered pretty things was distasteful.

"Is that sack a weapon? I've seen something like it before," I said.

"It is. People like obscure things. I often sell items like this to Miss Hatley."

"I've been in her cottage," I said. "It was an illuminating tour."

"She enjoys collecting odd things. These sacks were often filled with rubble or stone. They make an effective makeshift cudgel."

Had a sack like this been used to strike me? "Edmund gave you these items?"

"Yes, the plan was I'd sell them on and we'd split the profits."

"But you decided you didn't want to split the money, so you got rid of him?"

"I keep telling you, I had nothing to do with Edmund's death," Samuel said, growing irritated. "We made that arrangement before I stopped financing his project, but the deal still stood. I'd have given him his cut."

"But you wouldn't have been entirely honest about how much you charged for them?"

Samuel shrugged. "We all need to earn a living."

"Did you have a client in mind to sell these items to?"

"That's none of your concern."

"Would it have been a legitimate sale?"

"How I conduct my affairs is no matter to anyone but me."

Some of these finds would need to be declared as treasure, which meant Samuel should pay a portion of the profits as tax. It was no wonder he kept things quiet.

"Now Samuel is dead, who are you working with?" I asked.

"I work alone. It's better that way," Samuel said.

"You're working with a woman to uncover the missing Blackwood treasure."

"Why do you think that?"

"My dog fought back. He tore a piece of the attacker's clothing."

"Then why aren't you speaking to her?"

"Her identity is unknown, but I believe she was injured. Benji doesn't hold back when we're in danger."

"I'm glad you have such an effective attack dog," Samuel muttered, eyeing Benji warily. "But whoever this woman was, she has nothing to do with me. After my association with Edmund ended, I searched the tunnels myself. Edmund didn't own them, and I've invested time and money making some of them safe so I can keep looking."

"And slowly removing the competition as you go?" I asked.

"You've got the wrong end of the stick. I'm sorry you were injured, but I had nothing to do with it. Nor did my imaginary female partner. After I finished my digging, I headed back through the butcher's and stopped at the Green Man for a couple of pints before turning in. Ask your landlord. He'll confirm I was there."

"I'll be sure to do that," I said. "And while you're feeling open with the truth, where were you really on the night of Edmund's murder?"

"You're a nosy one. I see why you find yourself in so much trouble."

"You can tell me or the police. Unless you want to find yourself the chief suspect in this investigation, I'd advise you to give me the information."

"My shop may operate close to the legal line," Samuel said, "but I'm not in the business of killing people to get what I want. I make a good living selling rare items through certain channels that pay highly for discretion and efficiency. That night, I exchanged goods with a private client."

"And the name of that client?"

"Is confidential."

"Then you have no alibi. I'll inform the police. They will bring you in and—"

"Stop! I'll write it down. Just be discreet and do not mention Edmund's murder." Samuel furiously scribbled a name and thrust the paper at me.

"I shall say I'm looking for a reputable dealer and ask about your most recent transactions. We will not speak of the murder."

Samuel shook his head. "If you'll excuse me, I have work to do."

I didn't stop Samuel as he returned the items to the storeroom. I'd exhausted this line of questioning. I still thought little of the man, and I didn't admire his dubious business practices, but he'd been shocked to hear I'd been hurt. And he had no idea about the woman who'd followed me into the tunnel. Provided his new alibi checked out, I'd come to a dead end.

But if Samuel wasn't a murderer, then who was?

# Chapter 23

After my less-than-satisfactory meeting with Samuel, I was at a loss. My belief in Samuel's involvement in Edmund's murder had weakened after our conversation. I was in no doubt his business hadn't a legitimate bone in its dusty body. But a murderer? I wasn't so sure.

"Oh, good morning. It's Veronica, isn't it?" William's fiancée, Elizabeth, had almost stepped on me as she exited a smartly fronted haberdashery with a bundle of wrapped packages in her arms.

"It is. I see you've already had a busy morning." I nodded at the packages.

"There is so much to do when planning one's wedding, don't you think?" She grimaced and stepped from foot to foot.

"I really couldn't say. I'm not married."

"Gracious, at your age?"

My eyebrows shot up.

"Oh, please excuse my manners. But you're not an unattractive lady, and William has told me how clever you are. Although perhaps that's the problem. Some chaps don't like an intellectual woman. They find it intimidating." Elizabeth hopped from foot to foot again.

"Is something troubling you?" I asked.

"Would you mind taking my packages?" She held them out. "I have something in my shoe."

I took the packages and waited patiently as Elizabeth wriggled out of her dainty heel, tapped it lightly, and then peered inside.

"How frustrating. I see nothing, but there's something hurting my heel. I can't afford a blister." She thumped it again and ran her finger around the inside. "Perhaps it's a problem with the sole. I may have to discard these, which is a pity. I spent an age breaking them in." After she'd replaced her shoe, she took back the parcels.

"It's good to see you looking so much better," I said.

"Gracious, when have I ever not looked well?" Elizabeth looped an arm through mine in an over-friendly manner. "Shall we walk together?"

"Providing we're going in the same direction."

"I've seen you striding about town, so I know you're a walker." Elizabeth gently tugged me along with her.

"I enjoy the exercise," I replied. "As does Benji."

Elizabeth wrinkled her nose as she glanced at Benji. "Don't you find the dog fur exhausting? You must always be plucking it off your clothing."

"It doesn't bother me," I said. "Benji sheds little, and only when it's very hot."

Elizabeth ran a critical eye over my practical clothing. "William likes dogs, but I've said we can't have one. I'll be rushed off my feet, keeping everything spick and span as it is. And of course, when the children arrive, there'll be no time for a dog."

"That sounds fatiguing," I said.

"It's what's expected of us. William will soon be in charge of the bank, and I'll stay at home and look after our family."

"You'll be content with that?"

"I know my place. Women these days have more opportunities, but does it make them happy? What are you? Heading towards forty and still not married? No children, either. What a pity."

I smiled, unsure whether Elizabeth was attempting to vex me or had no filter for her thoughts. "I'm a fair way off forty. And I'm very comfortable in my relationship."

"Oh, that's right. William said something about you being married to an injured policeman."

"Gosh! You have done your homework."

She smiled. "Small towns. One has nothing to do but soak up the gossip."

"Well, you're not quite right with all the gossip you're gathered. I'm not married to Jacob, but he did work as a detective in London. After an injury, we went into business as private investigators."

"You? A detective? Perish the thought!"

"It's a perfectly reasonable thought," I said.

"Don't you want a home and children? It's not too late, you know, even at your advanced age."

"I have a comfortable home. I want for nothing."

"You'll change your mind. We all do. When I was young, I wanted to be a princess and spend my time riding around the countryside on horses. Then I met William. He made me realise where my skills are, and now I'm content planning our wedding and our future. Although... I do have a troubling situation to deal with."

"A problem with William?" I asked, still shocked by the woman's over-friendliness. Perhaps it had something to do with her thoughts being wholly occupied by marriage. I'd heard many brides-to-be claim they lost all sensibility when summoning the energy to wed.

"William is an angel. But I want to surprise him by finding him the perfect wedding band. I've looked everywhere and keep coming up empty-handed. It must be unique."

"Did you visit the antique shop this morning?" I asked.

"Oh! I did. Goodness me, you are a splendid detective," Elizabeth said. "How did you know? You're not following me, are you?"

"Samuel mentioned he dealt with a female customer just before I spoke to him."

Elizabeth stopped and glared at me. "Why are you speaking to Samuel? Are you looking for a ring, too?"

"Why would I desire a ring?"

"For your fiancé, of course."

"We're not engaged," I said. "And I have no interest in marriage."

She drew in a scandalised breath. "If you're not desiring marriage, he's not the man for you. But keep your hands off any antique rings you see. I want them for William."

"All of them?"

Elizabeth's sunny disposition vanished as fast as the coldness appeared. "I must find the perfect ring. My wedding must be flawless. Nothing can go wrong."

"All wedding rings are safe from me," I said.

Her eyes narrowed. "You clever types are always attempting to pull the wool over my eyes."

"You don't consider yourself clever?"

"I know my talents. Now, I must dash. I have an appointment with the hairdresser." She raced away, a ball of fizzing pre-marital jitters.

I watched Elizabeth until she turned the corner. She occasionally stopped and fiddled with her shoe, suggesting it still troubled her.

"Benji," I murmured. "We've found our missing puzzle piece. Who'd have thought it would be so highly strung?"

---

It was mid-afternoon when I found myself back in the Green Man pub, in front of all parties interested in learning who murdered Edmund Blackwood. Bishop's firm instruction, promising the killer's unveiling, convinced them all to attend.

Colin stood behind the bar after providing drinks to everyone. May Shaw stood next to Florence Hatley, while Samuel Drake stood to attention close to William Foster and his fiancée, Elizabeth. Bishop had escorted Charles Blackwood to the pub, although he was in handcuffs, since the police still stubbornly considered him the chief suspect.

"Thank you for coming, ladies and gentlemen," Bishop said. "We've had a development in the case and thought you'd be interested in learning the latest." He looked at me, where I stood waiting impatiently with Jacob and Benji to reveal all, and gestured for me to take the floor.

"Thank you. As you'll all be aware, Edmund Blackwood's body was found in the snug of this pub," I said, "a pub that belongs to my family. Given that, I was interested in finding out who was audacious enough to commit murder here and think they'd get away with it."

Samuel shifted uncomfortably, and no one else in the party looked happy.

"I'll start with the easiest suspect to dismiss. My landlord, Colin," I said. "The police were interested in him because he was here at the time of the murder. Edmund, who'd grown obsessed with finding the hidden Blackwood treasure, had bothered him for access to the smugglers' tunnel beneath this pub."

Colin grunted and vigorously polished an already clean spot on the bar.

I continued, "Colin tolerated Edmund because he paid him a little money to gain access to the tunnels."

"I've already admitted to that," Colin said. "I shouldn't have done it."

"The police believed Colin had a motive because Edmund became bothersome. They wondered if Colin snuck into the snug and walloped Edmund. But as witnesses in the pub testified, Colin couldn't have committed such a terrible crime." I smiled at him. "And having known Colin for many years, I say with confidence, he's an uncomplicated man. It would have been impossible for him to murder someone and return to business as usual."

"I'm happy to be called simple if it means I'm innocent," Colin said with a shrug.

"What about Charles?" Samuel asked. "He's been behind bars for days. He's an obvious choice."

I nodded. "Charles is the family's black sheep and got himself into hot water because of his gambling problem. He's lost everything. The police consider him a desperate man who turned to his brother for help. When Edmund denied him, they believe he lost control and murdered his brother to get his hands on the estate."

"It's a viable motive," May said. "All of us are aware of Charles's struggles. The man is homeless."

"And it's possible he would have been charged if he didn't have an airtight alibi," I said.

"I keep saying I'm innocent." Charles's voice was barely audible. "No one will listen. The police are telling me to confess."

"I'm glad you didn't. Because you are innocent. Mickey O'Rourke confirmed that, as did his men. You're no killer, Charles." I turned my attention to Florence Hatley. "For a time, I wondered about you, Miss Hatley. Your outward appearance is that of a frail old woman whose mind rests firmly in the past. But that past is tangled with the Blackwood family."

"I can't say I'm fond of them," Miss Hatley said stiffly. "They did my ancestors no good."

"And it's fair to say you still hold a grudge against them."

"I do. But I've already told you my alibi. I may be sprightlier than people give me credit for, but I'm not speedy enough to nip to this pub and clobber Edmund."

"The police contacted the lady who brought in your evening meal. She remembered you didn't have your shoes on that night, and you can't get them on without help, so it seems unlikely you'd wander across the cobbles in your stockings and commit the crime," I said.

"Indeed, I wouldn't. I may be eccentric, but I have my dignity!"

"You mentioned the O'Rourke family," William said. "Are they behind this?"

"No, but they provided Charles's alibi," I replied.

I turned to Samuel. "Let's focus on you for a moment."

"You know I'm not behind this," Samuel said. "We've sorted that."

"You have secrets to hide, but murder isn't one of them. Your dubious business activities will be investigated, but I checked the information you gave me and confirmed your whereabouts."

Samuel blew out a breath. "Then who is the killer? William? You've not interrogated him."

William looked appalled, while Elizabeth scowled at Samuel for daring to make such an inexcusable suggestion.

"I considered William a suspect because Edmund didn't like him," I said. "There was tension between them, and William covets the bank manager position, especially with his upcoming wedding looking to be quite the extravagant affair."

"I'd do nothing so base," William said, his voice low but firm.

"Fortunately for you," I replied, "the security guard at the bank confirmed where you were on the evening of the murder. But the matter of who is stealing from the bank has yet to be determined. And I suspect the police are very interested in you."

"My fiancé isn't a thief!" Elizabeth clutched William's arm. "We're a respectable couple."

I turned my gaze to her. "Are you?"

A hush settled across the room.

"A woman murdered Edmund." I turned to May.

May pressed a hand against her chest. "You cannot seriously think I killed him."

"Although you're a well-respected historian in this community," I said, "your ancestors also fell afoul of the Blackwoods' deceptions. They lost a fortune, and most were forced to flee to Australia and start again."

May narrowed her eyes. "How did you find that out?"

"Much like you, I adore an archive. Research is a hobby of mine."

May's lips thinned.

"Did you wish to preserve the family name?" I asked. "Or were you motivated to protect your place at the university? I suspect you were concerned that any scandal from your past, once revealed, would ruin your chance of becoming a professor."

May opened and closed her mouth just as Bishop stepped forward, his eyes locked on her.

But I held up a hand. "As solid a motive as May has, she didn't do it."

Samuel frowned. "Who does that leave? If a woman committed this crime, there are no more women left."

After my earlier conversation with Elizabeth, I realised I'd got everything wrong. I should have followed my instincts when considering how unstable planning a wedding made a person.

I turned, letting my gaze settle on the pretty woman with the cold eyes. "It was you."

# Chapter 24

Elizabeth gasped. "How dare you! I will not be spoken to like that. William, tell her!"

William shifted beside her. "Miss Vale, what do you mean by accusing my dear fiancée of such a terrible crime?"

"I'd like you all to expose your arms," I said.

A ripple of confusion spread through the group.

"Why should we do that?" May asked, even as she unbuttoned the cuff of her blouse.

"The person who murdered Edmund also harmed me," I said. "When I followed Samuel into a smugglers' tunnel, I was attacked and knocked out cold. Fortunately, my dog was fast on his paws and tore off a piece of my attacker's clothing and bit them. Whoever attacked me has an injured arm."

"I'm happy to show you any part of my body if it proves I'm innocent." Samuel was already rolling up his sleeves.

After a few grumbles and exchanged glances, the group complied, one by one, revealing their arms.

No bites.

No injuries.

Nothing.

"Miss Vale doesn't know what she's doing," Elizabeth said. "At first, she accuses me of murder and then makes me expose my arms to a room full of people I barely know. It's an insult to my dignity."

Several of the group nodded and eyed me warily.

"Do we have a problem?" Bishop murmured to me.

"Your legs!" I exclaimed. "Benji bit one of your legs."

"I am not exposing my legs in a room full of gentlemen!" Elizabeth blushed, her round cheeks reddening.

"I'm happy to show you my legs," May said.

"So am I," Miss Hatley added. "It'll give you all a thrill."

May wore a smart pair of trousers, which she hitched to the knee. Miss Hatley eagerly flipped up the hem of her long burgundy skirt. Neither lady had injuries on their calves.

"Elizabeth, that leaves you," I said.

"And as I stated, I will not show my legs to anybody."

"We could do this in private," I offered. "To protect your modesty."

"I strongly object," Elizabeth said. "It's a waste of our time and an insult to our reputations."

"Why don't we go into a private room?" William suggested.

"You can't be siding with this harridan!" Elizabeth exclaimed. "You're on my side. You must support me to prevent such an indignity."

"We're all on the side of justice," I said. "This will be over in a jiffy if you cooperate."

"It's a matter of principle." Elizabeth folded her arms across her chest and glared at me.

"Please, darling. For me," William said.

"If you refuse to show me your leg, I have more evidence," I said. "A piece of torn velvet fabric, most likely from a dress, the floral scent of perfume on that fabric, and a trail of sand, leading from the Green Man."

"What does sand have to do with any of this?" Samuel asked.

"On two occasions, I've seen collections of old weapons. Miss Hatley owns some, as does Samuel. I learned that people sometimes used small sacks filled with rubble, stone, or sand as improvised weapons. They could knock a person senseless. Maybe even kill them."

Samuel shrugged and nodded. "Do you think the sand was from an improvised cudgel?"

"When I discovered Edmund's body, Benji noticed a trail of sand leading out of the snug. A cudgel is an easy weapon to hide under a skirt or in a large purse. The killer trailed the sand behind them as they left. Perhaps the cudgel developed a hole after Edmund was struck."

"Which proves nothing about my guilt," Elizabeth said.

"Your shoe troubled you this morning," I said. "You thought you had a small stone or a problem with the sole, but you have sand in your shoe. It must have trickled in after you hit Edmund."

William reeled away from Elizabeth. "You've been complaining about a particular pair of shoes. Is that why?"

"Don't be so foolish," Elizabeth snapped. "The shoes were poorly made. I intend to return them to the shop and demand a refund."

"Those shoes weren't troubling you until recently," William said.

"Do be quiet!" Elizabeth hissed at him. "You know nothing of the trials a woman goes through to be appealing. Pinching heels, barely any food to maintain a trim figure, and primping. All the primping!"

"Police are searching your rooms as we speak," I said to Elizabeth. "They're looking for two things: the cudgel and a velvet dress with a piece of fabric missing. Do you think they'll find such a dress concealed somewhere?"

"What the devil! You have no right to interfere with my things," Elizabeth shrieked. "I did not give the police permission to violate my private quarters."

"Show Veronica your legs," Samuel said, a hint of glee on his face. "Otherwise, everyone will think you're guilty."

"I will do no such thing."

"Samuel, when we spoke this morning, you referred to me as another hysterical female. Was the first hysterical female you encountered today, Elizabeth?" I asked.

"Well, yes, it was," he said.

"And what was she seeking?"

"She's been coming in almost every day, demanding to see the wedding bands I have for men. I keep telling her I keep few in stock and only get a few now and again, but she keeps demanding something unique." He shook his head. "This morning, she was in tears, saying the wedding was almost here and she had to find something perfect. She said she'd do whatever it took to get it."

"There's nothing wrong with wanting the best for my husband," Elizabeth said. "If you ran a legitimate antique shop, instead of selling all that fake nonsense, you'd provide me with an appropriate service."

"Elizabeth is so focused on discovering the perfect wedding ring for William that she'd do anything to get her hands on one," I said. "Even following Samuel into a smuggling tunnel, hoping to see where he dug for treasure. She planned an excavation, intending to find a truly magnificent ring to give to her husband."

"You've been snooping on me?" Samuel asked Elizabeth.

"It was my bad luck that I was following Samuel that same evening," I said. "Elizabeth saw me, and fuelled with pre-wedding flutters, decided to get rid of potential wedding ring competition."

"This is ridiculous," May said. "Why would anybody get so het up over an outdated tradition?"

I barely suppressed a smile. "We're of the same mind, but there are ladies who favour marriage. For some, it's their singular ambition. Isn't that right, Elizabeth?"

"Your modern views will not embarrass me," Elizabeth said. "And I will find the perfect ring for William."

"You really should show us your legs," Samuel said. "When you came into my shop, I thought I'd have to call the police. You wouldn't leave until I showed you inside every cabinet because you thought I was hiding the wedding bands out of spite."

"I was being thorough," Elizabeth said.

"Darling, why not show your legs and get this business over with?" William had inched away from Elizabeth, and there was more than a hint of concern on his face.

"If we take you into custody, we can insist upon it," Bishop said. "Better to get it out of the way here."

"You don't want the police rough-handling you," Charles said. "I've experienced more than my fair share of that, and it's not pleasant."

Elizabeth's wide, panicked eyes swept around the room. "I will not be treated like a common criminal."

"Then you'd better not have acted like one," Colin said from behind the bar. "Show us your legs."

Elizabeth clutched the fabric of her floor-length pale-yellow dress. "Why aren't you helping me?" she hissed at William.

He gulped. "You must admit, you're obsessed with our wedding. The fabric. Food. Flowers. Everything you want, I simply can't afford it."

"Is that why you've been stealing from the bank?" I asked.

"William hasn't been stealing! Stop spreading lies with that vicious, bitter tongue. You're only like that because you're an unmarried old crone and no one wants you!" Elizabeth's tone was so shrill, I wouldn't be surprised if a pack of dogs burst into the pub.

William slid further away from Elizabeth. "I thought you were perfect, but ever since I proposed, you've changed. You keep buying things, adding more names to the guest list. The last sample menu you brought me had eight courses. How am I expected to afford that?"

"You said you'd provide for me," Elizabeth said. "You promised. Nothing will spoil my perfect wedding."

"Bleeding heck! She did it," Colin said. "She clobbered Edmund. You cunning creature."

"William! You will support me this instant and tell everybody I'm innocent!" Elizabeth demanded.

He shook his head, his gaze not meeting hers. "I... I can't do that. You're not of sound mind. You frighten me. You're always demanding more. I'm wrung out."

Elizabeth let out an ear-piercing shriek and rushed to the door. Before she could grab the handle, Benji was on her back. He slammed her into the door, roughly grabbed the neck of her dress, and pulled her to the floor before fiercely shaking her.

The tussle caused Elizabeth's dress to lift, exposing her right calf, where all could see an angry, red dog bite.

"Well, I'll be blowed," Miss Hatley said. "She was crazy enough to do it."

"There you go, Jacob," I said. "I've always said marriage invokes madness."

---

It was late evening, and I was enjoying a relaxing after-dinner drink with Jacob. Elizabeth had been arrested and formally charged with Edmund Blackwood's murder after admitting she'd do whatever it took to ensure her husband prospered. William had broken off the engagement, and although he was free of one nightmare, he faced police questioning over the theft from the bank. It was likely he'd lose his job and receive a custodial sentence.

Benji lay contentedly at my feet, gently snoring, no doubt feeling victorious at bringing down the deranged killer and the person who'd so viciously attacked me.

"Do you find normal life terribly dull?" Jacob sat across from me with his back to the open fire in the Green Man.

"I can't say I do," I said. "Why do you ask?"

"Your eyes never shine brighter than when you're in the middle of solving a murder," he said. "Then you come back to daily life. Writing obituaries, walking Benji, avoiding dealing with the troubles with Ruby..."

"My normal life is as frenetic as solving any crime," I said. "It will never be dull. Besides, you make life interesting."

"It's important to keep you on your toes," Jacob said. "Before you go back to London, spend a few days in Margate. I got that new job, and it looks interesting."

"I wish I could. But I know my mother's been phoning you daily. Sometimes twice a day," I said.

"Only because you don't return the messages she leaves at your lodgings."

"She knows I'm an independent woman. Besides, my mother is busy with Colonel Basil."

"About that..." Jacob leaned forward. "I spoke to Matthew the other day. He has concerns about Colonel Basil."

"I've heard the same," I admitted. "I've been meaning to look into him, but there never seems to be a spare moment."

"Let me do that. Save you the trouble," Jacob said. "From all accounts, your mother is happy, and I don't want you falling on her bad side by poking around in Colonel Basil's past and discovering nothing."

"Thank you. I'd appreciate that," I said. "You see? Normal life is as interesting as us solving a murder together."

"You practically solved this one on your own," Jacob said.

"I had help. Bishop was most obliging."

"He's a good sort," Jacob said. "He's had his troubles, but he's flourished since his fresh start down here."

"And of course, he has his good friend keeping an eye on him," I said.

"Isn't that what friends are for?" He gave me a pointed look.

"Talking of friends, I'm taking Jenny to see the dogs we rescued. She's looking for a four-legged companion to keep her company at the bed-and-breakfast. I think the small tan chap will be perfect for her."

"I didn't mean that sort of friend."

I was about to make a witty retort when the pub door was pushed open. Lady M stepped inside, magnificent in a burgundy gown, diamonds glittering at her throat. She paused, surveying the room.

The pub fell silent as everyone turned to look, struck by her statuesque and imposing presence. Lady M was used to such scrutiny and glided past tables without sparing anyone a glance or appearing self-conscious.

I stood to greet her. "Goodness, this is a surprise. Although it shouldn't be. You've been following Jacob and me."

She dismissed my words with a brisk wave of her hand. "I make no apologies for that."

I arched an eyebrow. "You make no apologies for skulking about after me?"

"I was checking on you. But I'm not here about that." Lady M drew in a shaky breath, and I suddenly noticed how tired she looked. "You must come with me. Ruby is gravely ill, and she's asking for you."

# Historical Notes

I have a fondness for the town of Faversham. I bought my first house there in my mid-twenties and would often walk out by the creek when in need of respite as my first grown-up relationship sadly fell apart.

I've also been in the Sun Inn (renamed the Green Man in this story) and enjoyed the charming historical surroundings.

The town has altered almost beyond recognition since I lived there, with large new housing estates growing around the core, but there is still a quaintness to Faversham, which I hope it always retains.

**Faversham:** With its intricate network of creeks and its proximity to the continent, Faversham was a prime location for smuggling for centuries. While the heyday of large, organised smuggling gangs in Kent was generally in the 18th and early 19th centuries, the activity continued in various forms into the 20th century.

Smuggling in Kent, including around Faversham, initially revolved around the illegal export of wool. High government taxes on wool made it profitable to ship it covertly to the continent. As import taxes on luxury goods like tea, spirits, and tobacco were introduced, the focus shifted to bringing these items into the country.

The 18th and early 19th century was the most notorious period for smuggling in Kent. The county's geography, with its muddy tidal creeks, sandy coves, and marshes, provided ideal landing spots. Faversham's inlets and creeks and well-hidden trails across the marshes made it fertile ground for the lucrative trade.

- **Organised Gangs:** While some smuggling was small-scale, Kent became home to ruthless, highly organised gangs. These groups were involved in everything from Jacobite rebellions to international espionage. They often transported goods in broad daylight, sometimes in convoys of heavily armed men, and were known for violence, bribery, and even murder.

- **Faversham's Role:** Daniel Defoe, writing in 1724, famously remarked that he knew nothing else Faversham was remarkable for "except the most notorious smuggling trade." The town's port, away from the major naval base at Sheerness, made it a convenient hub. Boat builders in Faversham, were known to construct the fast boats used by smugglers.

- **Low Key but Brazen:** Faversham's smugglers were often described as more 'low key' though still openly brazen. There's a notable account from 1821 where two captured smugglers, imprisoned in Faversham gaol, were sprung just days later when their gang attacked the prison with pickaxes and clubs.

- **Community Involvement:** Smuggling was often deeply embedded in the local economy and culture. Many communities connived in the trade, and wealthy individuals financed operations.

The end of the Napoleonic Wars and increased efforts by authorities (including the establishment of the Coastguard) led to a decline in large-scale, overt smuggling. Smuggling became less profitable as trade with the continent opened up and duties were adjusted. Many of the large gangs were broken up, with members hanged or transported.

While the dramatic, large-scale smuggling of the 18th century faded, smaller-scale illicit trade would likely have continued in Kent, including around Faversham, into the 1920s. The basic economic drivers for smuggling can persist, even if the methods become more clandestine. The winding creeks and rural areas offer opportunities for discreet landings and transportation of contraband, though perhaps not with the same level of open defiance seen in earlier centuries.

**The Green Man:** I took liberties with the pub names, renaming the Sun Inn in West Street in the historic heart of Faversham. It's a pub steeped in centuries of history, dating back to the 14th century. Its longevity and prominent location reflect its importance within the town's social and commercial life.

This pub has connections in the medieval period, with some sources suggesting it was built by Christ Church Priory in Canterbury around 1437-38 as a large pilgrim's hostel, given Faversham's position on a traditional route to Canterbury. This would have made it a vital stop for travellers and pilgrims seeking lodging. The building retains many original features, including inglenook fireplaces and exposed oak beams.

Like many historic inns in market towns, the pub thrived as a coaching inn during the 17th, 18th, and 19th centuries. This meant it provided not only food and drink but also accommodation for travellers, horses, and a hub for postal services and public transportation.

When the coaching inn era faded with the advent of railways and motor transport, the pub continued to operate as a pub and hotel. It adapted to changing times, but always maintained its historic character. In the 1920s, it would have been a well-established and recognisable landmark in Faversham.

# About the author

Immerse yourself into Kitty Kildare's cleverly woven historical British mysteries. Follow the mystery in the Veronica Vale Investigates series and enjoy the dazzle and delights of 1920s England.

Kitty is a not-so-secret pen name of established cozy mystery author K.E.O'Connor, who decided she wanted to time travel rather than cast spells! Enjoy the twists and turns.

Join in the fun and get Kitty's newsletter (and secret wartime files about our sleuthing ladies!)

**Newsletter:** https://BookHip.com/JJPKDLB
**Website:** www.kittykildare.com
**Facebook:** www.facebook.com/kittykildare